MISS POLLY HAD A DOLLY

WILLOW ROSE

Miss Polly had a dolly who was sick, sick, sick.

So she phoned for the doctor to be quick, quick, quick.

The doctor came with his bag and his hat
And he knocked at the door with a rat-a-tat-tat.
He looked at the dolly and he shook his head
and he said, "Miss Polly, put her straight to bed!"
He wrote on a paper for a pill, pill, pill
"I'll be back in the morning with my bill, bill, bill."

NURSERY RHYME

1

———

JULY 1997

Miss Polly loved her dolly. That's what she called her. *My Baby Doll.* Because her beautiful daughter looked just like a doll with her blue sparkling eyes and long blonde hair. And Miss Polly loved to dress her up, just like she was a small doll. She had done it ever since the child was born, but now that she had turned six years of age, she was beginning to resent her mother for doing so.

"I don't want to wear that dress, Mommy," she would say. "I want to wear pants like the other girls."

Pretty dresses weren't currently in style among little girls, and Miss Polly knew she soon faced the end of an era where she was able to decide what her daughter should wear. It wouldn't be long before her rapidly maturing daughter demanded to decide on her own. Miss Polly knew that, and therefore, she tried to enjoy it while it lasted. This morning she put three different dresses on her little girl and took pictures of her in all of them. Each outfit complete with matching headbands, of course.

"The light blue one is the prettiest," she said and looked at her gorgeous daughter.

Miss Polly had never been beautiful or even remotely pretty as a child, and her own mother hadn't cared about anything other than teaching Miss Polly how to cook, so she could be sent away as a maiden at the tender age of thirteen.

So that was her excuse for dressing up her baby girl every day, even if it was only to take her to the playground, like today, and show her off to all of the other mothers.

"You ready?" she asked and put on her hat.

Her daughter appeared behind her. Miss Polly couldn't help but smile when she saw her. She walked to her and set her dress straight and then washed a small smudge off her face by licking her thumb and carefully wiping at it.

"Now there. I think we're ready."

Miss Polly opened the door and let her daughter walk out first. Then they started parading down their street, hand in hand, enjoying the many looks from neighbors and passersby, whose eyes always smiled when they landed on the little girl. Miss Polly could see in them how beautiful they thought her daughter was and felt a thrilling sensation of pure joy in her stomach.

Her little angel of a doll had given her many hours of that kind of joy ever since she had come into her life. The father, they never spoke of. Miss Polly had told her to never ask about him, since he wasn't important to either of them any longer. The fact was that he had run off as soon as Miss Polly had told about the baby. At first, he had told her that he wanted her to take care of it, to terminate the pregnancy, but Miss Polly had refused that with a snort. At age thirty-seven, she knew this might very well be her last chance to have a child.

"Then I don't want anything to do with it," he had said angrily.

"You don't have to," Miss Polly had answered. "We don't need you or any other man for that matter."

"Good."

Then he got up from the kitchen table in the small apartment that she had rented back then and left. She hadn't heard from him since, and she hoped she never would. They were doing fine on their own, her and her angelic little girl. No need for a third party to ruin the fun.

"Three is a crowd," Miss Polly always said. And it was so true.

When they reached the playground she felt the other women's jealous eyes on her daughter. Miss Polly kneeled in front of her and held her hands in hers.

"Now remember, no getting dirty in there. You're wearing your prettiest dress. Pretty girls don't get dirty. Don't you forget that, my child."

"But the other children..."

"You're not like those other children, sweetheart. You're very special. Some day the entire world is going to admire your beauty, and when they do, you'll be prepared for it. Let them look at you, but don't let them get too close."

"But how am I going to play if I can't get dirty or get close to the other kids?" her daughter said with a petulant whine.

"No. No. Pretty girls don't whine, either, my lovely. Or frown for that matter. And don't crinkle your nose like that. It's not becoming. You'll end up getting wrinkles at an early age. Remember, it's all about keeping up appearances, *Baby Doll*. Now go."

Miss Polly drew in a satisfied breath and looked on as her daughter walked towards the playground in her ballerina shoes, taking small feminine steps just like she had taught her to.

2

APRIL 2013

"This book is based on events that happened to me and my family last year. It is the true story of those events in my own words."

I looked down at the cover of my book, *Itsy Bitsy Spider*, then out on the crowd gathered in front of me. All eyes were on me, expecting me to entertain them, explain to them what really happened and if it *really could be true?* That was the question I got the most at these book signings. People found it hard to believe that all this really had taken place, that all this could have happened to one person, one family.

But it did. None of us had forgotten what happened only six months ago when we were all almost killed by Fanoe Island's first serial killer, and now I had written a book about it. Only a month after it had hit the stores, it had become a national best-seller, much to my surprise. Everybody loved the story, and even though the critics hated it, I was selling a lot of books around the country.

I opened the front cover and started reading out loud. I had been all over the country in the last month doing book signings, but this was a special one for me. This took place at the local bookstore in downtown Nordbo, the town that had become my hometown after my grandmother died and left me her house. I started reading out loud, thinking about my dad, who had promised me he would come to hear me today, but hadn't arrived just yet, much to my disappointment. Well, he knew the story the book was based on a little too well, so maybe he would peek in later.

I spotted my son Victor and my daughter Maya in the crowd. Victor didn't seem to enjoy being in the crowd too much. He suffered from a form of light autism that the doctors couldn't quite place or put a diagnosis on, but being in a crowd was among the things he didn't cope with too well. My daughter, Maya, didn't look too pleased, either. On our way down here she had explained to me that she found it so embarrassing that her mom was on a poster outside the bookstore, and even worse that I was going to be talking about our family and what had happened. She hated the fact that I had written a book with her in it, and even more that everybody in the country seemed to have read it.

"It's so embarrassing, Mom," she had told me when I told her what the book was about. "Everybody is going to know all kinds of stupid things about us. Why exactly do you feel the need to tell them all these things about our family?"

"Because I'm a writer, that's why. It's a great story and I need to tell it."

I had changed the names, but still she had never forgiven me for writing it. Not even when I told her that with the advance we got I would be able to buy her a new iPad. She had never been easy to bribe, unfortunately for me.

I read out loud from the first chapter of the book that I was so proud of. I glanced up at the audience in between paragraphs. As I did, I spotted Jack, one of my neighbors from across the road and couldn't help but smile at seeing him in the crowd. My friend Sophia, who also lived across the road from me, was standing next to him, trying hard to hear me read while two of her kids pulled her arms. She was carrying her newborn in a sling on her front. She looked exhausted, but smiled anyway, which I thought was quite the accomplishment, having six kids and being alone with all of them.

I finished the reading then looked out at the many people that had come to hear me. Then I smiled and nodded and received my applause. It was mostly tourists, I noticed, but that was no surprise to me, since not many people from the island had liked the idea of me publishing this book. I was constantly receiving remarks, especially from church people who felt they were being put on display in my book, which I admitted they were, but frankly that wasn't my fault. They had done some horrible things in the past and some of them had paid for it with their lives. That was the story and I couldn't change it.

"Now, I'll do book signings over by the table," I said and moved over to the corner where the nice lady named Isabella Petersen who owned the store had put up a table and a chair.

She was the first and only bookstore owner on the island who had dared to agree to a book signing by me, and I was very thankful to her for that. I had asked my dad to bring her a basket of flowers and wine as a way of showing my gratefulness, so I was getting anxious now that he wasn't going to make it.

A line formed in front of the table and I started signing the books one by one.

"Who is it for?" I asked.

"Me. My name is Alice."

"Okay, Alice," I said and signed the book *To Alice, Hope you'll enjoy your reading. Best, Emma Frost.*

After signing about fifty or so, I finally heard my dad's voice behind me. He was out of breath when he spoke.

"Got the basket. I added some chocolate, I heard she likes that," he said and put the basket down next to me. It was nicely wrapped in cellophane. It was perfect.

"Where did you hear that?" I asked, thinking that it didn't matter, all women liked chocolate, right?

Another reader put her book on the table in front of me.

"Sign it to Gerda," she said with a German accent.

"My new girlfriend told me."

"Your what?" I stopped signing and looked up at my dad who was standing next to me and now I realized he was accompanied by a middle-aged woman with very red hair.

"Emma, meet Helle. Helle, this is Emma."

3

JULY 1997

Nina heard the ice cream truck from far away. She turned to look in the direction of the sound, but none of the other kids seemed to hear it. She looked in between the houses nearby to see if she could spot it.

Oh, how she would like to get an ice cream for once. Nina looked in her mother's direction. She was sitting on a bench smiling while keeping an eye on Nina, making sure she didn't get dirty or behave in an unsuitable way for a young girl.

Nina snorted. She was so sick and tired of having to act in a certain way and dress the way her mother directed her to. It took forever every morning for her mother to pick the right dress. When would she get it through her head that Nina didn't care about those things? Nina wanted to be able to play and get dirty like the rest of the kids. She liked wearing pants and a T-shirt and dreamed of the day she'd be able to convince her mother to buy her a pair of jeans. Nina sighed and smiled at her mother. No, that would probably never happen.

"Little girls should have long hair and wear pretty dresses," her mother always said whenever Nina dared bring up the subject.

Her mother could spend hours just brushing Nina's hair before bedtime. "A hundred strokes a day makes your hair beautiful."

Oh, how Nina loathed it when she called her beautiful or pretty. So many times she had wished that she wasn't pretty, that she could just look ordinary like the other kids. She had even once tried to cut her hair off, thinking that if she didn't look pretty then her mother would get off her back.

But her mother had caught her in the bathroom after she had cut off the first piece of hair.

"What are you doing to yourself!" She could still hear her yelling. And the yelling didn't stop for days. Every time she saw Nina she would start in again. "How dare you. You are blessed with such beautiful hair. Do you know how many small girls would die to have what you have, well do you? You should be grateful that God has given you such a gift. You should cherish it and honor it. Aren't you glad that you're not ugly like those other children?"

"I want to be ugly, Mom. I don't like being pretty!" she had said and run off to her room.

That didn't go down so well with her mother. The next week, Nina wasn't allowed to go outside or watch any of her favorite TV shows, or even read the magazines that her mother had bought for her, with pretty little girls on the front covers.

Not that Nina cared much about them, though. To be honest, she found them to be stupid. Nina had, on several occasions, asked her mother to bring her magazines with horses or tigers, which were the things she was really interested in, but her mother wouldn't hear of it, of course.

Since then, Nina hadn't attempted to cut her hair again. She did, however, dream of the day when she got to decide for herself what to wear and what to look like. When that day came, she was determined that she was never going to wear dresses again. Ever. Her mother would be devastated, but Nina didn't care. She had gotten her way while Nina was young; sooner or later, Nina would get her way, as well—whether her mother liked it or not.

A boy approached Nina on the playground with a smile. "Do you want to play?"

Nina shook her head, then looked in the direction of her mother. She was shaking her head as well and signaling Nina to *let him admire you, but don't let him come too close.*

"No. I'm sorry. I can't," she said. "I'm not allowed to."

The boy shrugged. "Why did you come to a playground, then?"

"To be seen," Nina said, putting her nose in the sky the way her mother always wanted her to. "At least that's what my mom calls it."

The boy shrugged again. Nina looked down at her shiny ballerina shoes. A touch of sand had landed on the top of them. Nina gasped, knowing how angry mother would be if she noticed, then she bent down and wiped it off. When she raised her head and looked at her mother, she noticed that she was staring at her. Nina smiled to show everything was fine and her mother's shoulders came down. Nina looked down at her dolly in her hand. *Little Miss Jasmine*, they called her. Nina hated that dolly. It had blue eyes just like she did and wore a pretty dress. Nina suddenly felt like throwing it far away.

The ice cream truck rang its bell again. Nina looked up and spotted it on a neighboring street. She looked over at her mother and wondered if she dared to ask her for ice cream once again.

No, not after what happened the last time.

Nina's mother didn't let her have ice cream—or anything else she considered unhealthy—since she needed to watch her weight and maintain a healthy complexion. Apparently, that was very important in life. Her mother had never taken care of herself and *see what she looked like now?*

Nina didn't care. She thought her mother looked fine. Once she had considered cutting her face, scarring her cheeks, to get her mother off her back, but she wasn't allowed to play with knives or scissors ever since that incident with her hair.

The bell rang again and Nina was getting hungry. She was sick of having salads for lunch and never having any dessert. She wanted ice cream and candy like normal kids. Nina looked at her mother again and noticed that another woman had approached her and they were now talking.

"Probably talking about me, how *adorable* I look," she mumbled to herself bitterly, thinking that would be the only reason for her mother to want to talk to any stranger that approached her.

Nina looked in the direction of the ice cream truck again, then made her decision. On her way across the lawn, she dropped Little Miss Jasmine and never cared enough to go back and look for her.

Nina stormed in between the houses and ended up on a small street. She spotted the ice cream truck a little further down the road and ran towards it. It had stopped and was ringing its bell. Nina was out of breath when she caught up with it. A woman stuck her head out and smiled.

"Hi there, you pretty little thing. Would you like some ice cream?"

Nina wasn't supposed to talk to strangers, so instead she just nodded.

"Look at the sheet and see if there's anything you'd like," the lady said and blew a bubble with her gum.

Nina pointed at the biggest one with most chocolate on it.

"Ah, that one, huh? Nice choice," the lady said. Then she disappeared for a while and came back and handed Nina the nicely wrapped ice cream. The golden wrapping was sparkling in the sun. It had a picture of the ice cream on the outside of it. Nina couldn't remember ever feeling happier than in that moment.

"That'll be ten kroner," the lady said.

At once Nina froze. Money. She hadn't thought about money. She felt how the blood left her body when she realized that the dream of ever tasting this small piece of heaven was still as far away as it had always been.

"I...I...I don't have any money."

Nina was ready to give the ice cream back and walk with a bowed head back towards her mother, who was probably angrier than ever now.

"You don't have any money?" the lady said and tilted her head. She chewed heavily on that bubblegum. "Well, you know what?"

Nina looked up with her big blue eyes. Was there still a way? Was there still a possibility that she might get the ice cream after all?

The lady looked to the sides, then whispered. "Come around the back. I have some extra that we usually don't sell, but keep for ourselves to eat."

Nina nodded eagerly, and gave the glittering ice cream back to the lady who winked at her before she closed the hatch to the magic ice cream truck. Nina looked carefully around to make sure her mother was nowhere to be seen, then walked behind the truck. The lady opened the back door, and peeked out.

"Come on inside; it's in the back."

Nina felt like she had somehow found an escape-way to heaven and was filled with excitement as she took the first step inside the truck. The smell inside was incredible, she thought, and she never noticed the door being locked behind her.

It wasn't until the truck started moving that she realized she wasn't going to taste the ice cream any time soon.

4

____

APRIL 2013

Patrick felt like he was losing control again. It scared him a little, but also filled him with excitement. The frightening part was that he sometimes found it hard to know what was reality and what was his fantasy. Patrick had always had many fantasies, but lately he had begun living and acting them out, and that caused him to lose control of reality from time to time. Simply because he slipped into a world of his own, and then there was no knowing what he was up to.

He looked at the Asian woman he had just picked up from the street. She was small, and he liked them small. He liked them young too, but he couldn't always get everything, now could he?

He accelerated in the small BMW convertible that the TV-station had rented for him while he was in town.

What town was it again? Viborg, that's right. Gotta keep

track of what's going on around you, Patrick. Can't lose complete control.

As usual, they were only in for a week, then off to a new town. It was like that all throughout the season of the show. Patrick loved it when a new season started and they toured around the country. It was the third year the TV show had aired, and every year it grew more and more successful. The first three episodes this spring had had the highest ratings any reality show on Danish television had ever had, so it was fair to say it was a success. He was a success. Patrick had been the host of the show since the beginning, and his face was synonymous with it to the viewers. When he walked out the door, he represented the TV show, they told him. They expected him to act like it.

"Where are we going?" the Asian girl asked with a slight shiver when she noticed they were leaving town.

"I know a place outside of town," he said. "More private like that."

The Asian girl closed her mouth and nodded. Patrick looked at her voluptuous lips. They were painted pink. Patrick didn't like that, he didn't care much for pink; in fact, it gave him the creeps. He found a napkin and handed it to her.

"Here, wipe that lipstick off. I don't like it."

She did as he told her. Now that was much better. Now her lips looked real. He had offered her two hundred for an hour. Figured she wasn't worth much more. She had accepted and jumped in his car without anyone seeing Patrick's face. He always made sure to use a back entrance when he left the hotel where his fans camped along with the paparazzi, and he disguised his face by wearing a hat or a hood from his sweater, since he was, after all, representing the TV show. The girl had recognized him once she was in the car, naturally, but that didn't matter.

She was never going to be able to tell anyone anyway.

Patrick spotted the right place, a rest area far enough from town to be completely left in darkness at night. Not a soul would ever see them. Patrick was beginning to feel worked up, almost high, at the thought of what was about to happen. It wasn't something he was able to control, it just kind of happened, came over him, like a wave inside of him. It was a rush of emotions, of manic ecstatic feelings that got him so high he could no longer control himself.

"What are we doing here?" the Asian girl asked, as he took the exit towards the rest area. Patrick turned off the car's headlights and let it roll into the area. It was empty alright, just as he had expected it to be. He found a spot and parked the car. The Asian girl looked at him and smiled. He could see the contrast of her white teeth on her brown skin in front of him. He fought the urge to knock them out, to smash her face in.

"So, you want to do it here?" she asked with an accent.

"Yes, I *want to do it here*," he repeated, mocking her accent.

"Okay," she said and took off her small jacket that barely covered anything. She was chewing gum and blowing bubbles while arranging her stockings.

"So, what do you want to do first? Do you want me to blow you or do you want to get inside of me right away? Remember, I don't do anal. That's off limits. But tell me your fantasy and I'll try and make it come true. After all, you *are* my first celebrity."

She blew another bubble. It annoyed Patrick immensely. Patrick reached over and grabbed her neck. She shrieked. He put his fingers into her mouth and pulled the gum out, then dropped it in her hair. With a finger he pressed it into her thick black hair.

"Hey!" she yelled and tried to remove it, but it was already stuck. Now it was on her fingers as well. "Do you have any idea how difficult it will be to get that kind of thing out of my hair? That's gonna cost you extra. At least fifty more."

Patrick laughed manically.

"You think it's funny, do you? Well, it's not. Why are you being so mean? I always thought you were a nice guy. You seem so sweet on TV," she said, pouting now.

Barely had she finished the sentence before Patrick couldn't hold himself back anymore and he punched her in the mouth, hoping it would make her shut up. She screamed and spat out a tooth. Blood was gushing from her mouth. She seemed dizzy from the blow. Her lip was broken and bleeding, too. Her head was spinning and her eyes were rolling up like she was about to fall unconscious. Patrick laughed, mainly because he was happy that he had finally made her shut up. Then he leaned over and kissed her, licked off the blood from her lips and drank from her. She tried to push him away, but her small Asian arms were powerless. Patrick fumbled with his hand in his pants and pulled out his knife. She didn't see it, but protested slightly when he leaned over and held her down. Very close to her ear, he whispered:

"This is my fantasy."

5

———————

APRIL 2013

I had no idea what to say. My dad had taken me and the kids out for lunch after the book signing, along with his new girlfriend, who I had heard nothing about up until today.

"So, Emma. It's so exciting with your book, huh?" the woman said.

I was eating my sandwich and had my mouth full when she asked. I stared at her while chewing, not knowing what to say to her. That I was in state of complete shock? That I had no idea she even existed? That I had seen my dad at least three times a week since he moved to the island to be closer to us, but he hadn't once mentioned her name? That I thought she looked like an old version of Pippi Longstocking? What? What do you say in a situation like this?

"Well, not everybody finds it so exciting on this island," I answered.

"Helle is not one of them," my dad said.

"Are you a newcomer like us?" I asked.

She shook her head. "I've lived here all my life. But I was never part of the church. My parents stayed away from all that."

"That's good to hear," I said and smiled. She seemed nice. I especially liked her eyes, and I was certain that once I got over the shock, I would be ready to give her a chance. At least my dad suddenly seemed very happy, almost cheerful, and that was a new approach for him, so maybe, just maybe she could do what my mother never accomplished? Could she be the one to make my dad happy finally? I wanted him to move on from my selfish mother, who had left him to move to Spain with some guy that I just hated. I wanted him to be happy again, to be at peace and enjoy his life.

I opened my mouth and took another bite of my sandwich, still while staring at her and her very red hair, her fluttering orange dress, and her many rings and bracelets. She had that look of an artist or a writer, and I couldn't help but admire her slightly for daring to stand out like that.

"Your children are beautiful," she said.

I looked at Maya and Victor, who were both eating in silence. I guessed they were just as surprised as I was. "I know," I said and smiled. "I'm very lucky." I ate more of my sandwich, feeling proud of my children. They had both been doing well in school all spring, even Victor had improved, his teacher said. He was interacting with the other children, and that was a huge step for him. Maya had gotten good grades and a new best friend named Annika, who she spent most of her time with. She was growing up to be such a great girl.

"Do you have any children?" I asked Helle, when I was done

chewing. I washed it down with a Coke that I wasn't supposed to have, since I had once again started a diet, and this time I really meant it.

Helle smiled awkwardly. "My daughter is no longer with us."

I almost choked on my ham. "My God. What happened?" I cleared my throat. "If you don't mind talking about it, that is?"

My dad put his arm around Helle's shoulder. "Maybe another day," he said.

Helle put her hand on his arm. "No, it's okay. I don't mind talking about it." She drew in a deep breath. I stopped eating, sensing this was too serious a subject. Helle's lips became tight, her eyes moist. "We think she drowned. It's the only explanation they have been able to come up with after all these years. But sometimes kids run out into the ocean by Fanoe Vesterhavsbad and get lost. When it is low tide you can walk to an island there and then they are surprised when high tide comes rushing in. They never found any trace of her, though. Not her body or even a piece of clothing, and I have no idea what she was doing out there without me knowing it. Last time I saw her we were at a playground, when I looked away for one second to talk with another mother, she was gone. The police think she might have run down to the beach not far from there and then walked into the water, thinking she could reach the island, Soren Jessen's Sand. *Maybe she wanted adventure*, they said. But my girl was never adventurous, not like that."

I looked at the woman and suddenly felt the deepest sympathy for her. I put my hand on her arm. "That's terrible, Helle."

She nodded and bit her lip. "I know. Took me many years to accept that she was gone and wasn't going to come back through the front door with some fantastic story about how she'd gotten lost but found her way home. Her father wasn't in our lives. She was all I had. But now I have finally learned to live with it. I still can't help myself, though, when I see a girl that looks like her or looks the way I think she would today. I guess I'm always on the lookout for her. I don't know if it'll ever stop."

"How old was she?"

"Six. She had just turned six years old."

6

—————

JULY 1997

"Your daughter is very lovely," the woman who had approached Miss Polly said. Miss Polly didn't care much about talking to strangers and always told Nina to never do so. But when they complimented her only true love in this world, her beautiful daughter, Miss Polly could never resist answering them.

"Yes, isn't she?" Miss Polly replied happily.

The woman rocked the stroller. Miss Polly could hear a baby fussing inside of it.

"How old is she?" the woman asked.

"Six. She just turned six years old."

"Gonna be some heartbreaker for the boys, huh?" The baby was fussing again and the woman rocked the stroller a bit more forcefully while hushing it. Miss Polly stared at the woman, feeling her heart accelerate. It was the word she had used. *The boys*. Miss Polly strongly resented the very idea of her precious

little girl having anything at all to do with those disgusting...
filthy creatures.

Boys. They only want one thing from you. And once you have given it to them, they leave you.

Miss Polly knew the day would come when she would have to face this problem with her Dolly. Up until now, she had merely decided that her daughter was never going to be with any boys when she reached her teens. Miss Polly simply wouldn't allow her to be with them. But deep inside, she knew that it was going to be a fight that she might end up losing eventually.

Just the thought of one of them...touching her. Defiling her. I won't let her be besmirched by them. I simply refuse to let that happen.

"So will she start school after the summer?" the woman asked.

Miss Polly was pulled abruptly out of her thoughts. She shook her head. "No, I will be homeschooling her."

"Homeschooling? That's unusual," the woman said.

Miss Polly was getting tired of this conversation and wanted the lady to leave now. All those questions were annoying and tiresome. But she was right. Miss Polly knew it was very unusual in Denmark for people to homeschool their children. It was mostly people who had children with severe autism or other disabilities, and even those had help. Miss Polly was going to do this completely on her own. Even if she had no idea how to do it. There was no way her precious baby doll was going to go to those noisy, filthy places called schools and be blemished by all those other dirty, filthy children. No, she was staying home where it was safe for her to be, where Miss Polly could watch her every moment.

"Yes, well that's what I've decided," she answered a little harshly, in the hope that the woman would go away if she sensed Miss Polly wasn't enjoying the conversation. But, apparently, the woman had no sense of decorum or any sense at all for that matter. She kept right on talking.

"That's really difficult, isn't it? I mean you have to follow a program or something, right? To make sure the child is taught the exact same as the rest of the children. And what about the social skills? How will she learn how to be a team player?"

Miss Polly looked into the woman's eyes while the anger rose in her.

Stupid Danish people. Always talking about everybody being equal, all that socialism is destroying our beautiful country. Don't they see it?

"My daughter will not be a team player," she burst out, knowing very well that her opinion was not like most people on the island, or even in the country. "She is special and I will raise her to know that. She will not go out and be ordinary; she will do many incredible things in life, and when she is a grown up everybody will know who she is, since she stood out in the crowd, since she is special and not like all the others. See, I do not believe we are all born to be equal. I believe some are destined for greatness. Now, if you'll excuse me, I will take my child home before she catches the bug of mediocrity that has become so common these days."

Miss Polly snorted and stood up in front of the woman.

"I'm sorry," the woman said and held a hand up in the air. "I was just trying to make conversation. Geez."

But Miss Polly was no longer listening. She stormed past the woman and towards the children playing. She tried to spot Nina amidst all the noisy children running around, but she couldn't see her anywhere.

Where are you, baby doll? You're not running around getting dirty like all those common children, are you?

Miss Polly was walking faster now while scanning the playground area. "Nina?" she called out, thinking she might be standing somewhere where she could not see her. Miss Polly searched under the slide and on the swings. There was no sign of her precious baby doll anywhere. Now her heart was racing rapidly and she had to put a hand to her chest to calm her breathing down. Where could she have gone? Miss Polly saw the boy that had been talking to Nina earlier and stormed towards him.

"Where is Nina? Where is the girl you talked to earlier?"

The boy looked at her indifferently and shrugged. "I don't know."

Miss Polly grabbed his shoulders and started shaking him, "Where is she? Tell me immediately. What have you done to her, you filthy animal?"

The boy started screaming and a couple of parents ran towards them. They pulled Miss Polly away from the boy. "What's the matter with you?" a woman said to her. Probably his mother, she had the same ugly nose. The ugly mother looked at Miss Polly disapprovingly, but she didn't care. It didn't matter. They didn't matter. All that mattered was finding her precious baby girl before it was too late, before someone...*Don't even think it*...the very thought of someone harming her felt like knives in her body. She could hardly bear it.

"He has done something to my girl. I can't find her," she said. "Where is she?" she yelled at him.

The boy whimpered while his mother put her arm around him and pulled him away. Miss Polly felt the playground start spinning. Could it be the woman that had been talking to her? She'd seemed a little too fond of Nina. Miss Polly started spinning to see if she could spot the woman, but she too seemed to have vanished.

What is happening here? Where is my girl?

Miss Polly was hyperventilating now and could hardly breathe. She bent over and took in a few breaths, while feeling very dizzy. Her poor weak heart couldn't take this. When she lifted her head to start the search again for her precious baby doll, she spotted *it* in the grass. Miss Polly gasped and ran across the lawn. She was panting and pushing kids aside who got in her way. Parents were yelling at her, telling her to *get the heck out of the playground, you crazy woman.* But Miss Polly didn't hear them. Her eyes were fixated on one small thing in the grass.

Little Miss Jasmine.

Miss Polly was crying hysterically when she picked her up. She held the doll close to her chest while crying.

"Where is she, Little Miss Jasmine? Where did she go?" she mumbled, while the tears ran down her cheeks. It felt so good to hold the doll again, just like when Nina had been a baby and Miss Polly would hold her in the exact same way. She held her tight to her body while desperately scanning the area surrounding them. Her lip was quivering and her tears falling to land on the doll's face. Miss Polly wiped the tears away from the doll's face with her hand.

"Can you believe it, Little Miss Jasmine? Can you? Miss Polly can't find her dolly."

7

———————

APRIL 2013

"Why didn't you tell me you were seeing someone?" I asked my dad when we got back to the house. Helle had to go back to her shop where she sold trinkets or something like that, according to my dad, who apparently didn't really know what it was she was selling.

"I don't know," he said and sat in a chair while I served him a cup of coffee. "I thought it would be better this way."

"You mean a sneak attack on one of my most important days?" I asked with a chuckle.

My dad laughed. "Yeah, something like that."

I found a box of Danish butter cookies and gave him a couple with his coffee. I grabbed a handful myself and started eating them.

"So, what did you think of her?" he asked with his mouth full.

I swallowed mine and drank some coffee while choosing my words carefully. "She seemed very nice, actually. I like her."

"Actually? You didn't expect to like her?"

I shrugged. "To be frank, no. It was quite a shock at first, and then I guess I reacted with resentment. But lunch was a good idea. Talking to her made me like her. But, I have to say, you didn't give her a fair chance bringing her like that. It wasn't fair towards her. You could have at least told me about her."

He ate another cookie and nodded. "Well, I was afraid you'd be angry, so I thought we should just get it over with."

I chuckled again. "You're impossible. You're lucky she still likes you after that stunt. That proves to me she's a good woman."

My dad smiled in a strange fashion. There was something about him.

Something...like...glowing? Could you say that about a guy? Well, he was glowing. He was happy and I don't think I had ever seen him happy before, not like this. It made me a little jealous. I think a little might be an understatement. Why wasn't I able to make him happy like that?

"She's a great woman," he said with that strange smile on his face. My dad never smiled much. He was grumpy about work, about his medical clinic when I was a child, he was angry at my mom for leaving him and moving to Spain the last few years, there had always been something for him to be moping about. But not now. Now he wasn't even grumbling. That was very new to me and a little odd, when I've become accustomed to such different behavior. Thinking about it while sitting in front of him, he had been a lot happier lately. I had just thought it was because of him finally being able to retire from his clinic and moving closer to his daughter and grandchildren.

I smiled with a sigh. "Well, as long as she makes you happy, Dad, then I am too. We should invite her over for dinner and get to know her a little better. If she is going to be in your life, then we should make her welcome."

My dad grabbed the paper and nodded. "Sounds great, sweetheart."

His face disappeared behind the local Fanoe paper where pictures from the TV show *Shooting Star* were plastered all over. *Shooting Star* was a TV reality show that featured children singing. A little like *X-factor* and those kinds of shows, only for children. It was the biggest talk of the island these days. The TV show was coming to Fanoe for the first time, and everybody wanted their kids to audition. The show's host was a young guy in his twenties who simply went by the name of *Patrick*. He was the most talked about host in Danish history, a horrible drama queen and prima donna, but always fun to watch. Especially when he whined excessively into the microphone in enthusiasm.

He *was* the show and most people liked to see the children sing, but they watched it because of him. He was funny, witty, and very, very handsome. And he wasn't afraid of acting crazy. People never knew what he would do or say next, and I had a feeling neither did the producers. He always did or said something that created headlines everywhere and made people talk. That made it the most popular show in Danish television history. Me, unlike most people my age, I wasn't afraid to admit it. I liked to watch *Shooting Stars* and I was definitely going to go down there for the auditions. Just to see the set-up, I didn't have any children that wanted to do it, but Sophia did. She had six kids in total and she had managed to persuade two of them to audition for the show. I was naturally going to be there to support her, and of course, hopefully catch a glimpse of the spectacular host.

8

———

APRIL 2013

Josephine Gyldenstjerne knew she was born for greatness. She also knew children weren't born equal and that she was among the few born to rule others. At the age of six, Josephine knew all about class distinctions and she knew her place in this world. As the daughter of a Count and Countess of Denmark, she knew she was destined to live a life of luxury.

As always in the spring, the family moved to the small island of Fanoe and lived at their residence close to the beach. And as always, Josephine was followed closely by her governess, Ms. Camilla, even when they took a rare break from her schooling and walked to the beach. Josephine adored the beach. She loved the mighty dunes and wide stretch of sand, and she particularly loved the huge ocean with nothing but water as far as you could see. Every afternoon this week she had begged Ms. Camilla to take her down there and watch the waves coming in from afar. And every day Ms. Camilla had said no, they had work to do. Until this Wednesday afternoon, when the sun was shining from a clear blue sky and even Ms. Camilla felt the calling of the birds and the alluring spring outside of the windows of the mansion they called their vacation residence.

"England is on the other side of the ocean," Ms. Camilla said, when they stopped at the top of the dunes. She pointed to make sure Josephine watched.

But Josephine didn't care. She knew all that and even more. She closed her eyes and breathed in the salty air blowing in from exotic places far, far away. She imagined a small boy at the shore in England standing just like she was and breathing in the same air, just hours earlier before it blew across the North Sea. She chuckled at the thought and opened her eyes. Ms. Camilla was still talking about England and trying to teach her stuff that she already knew. Josephine had spent most of her life reading and learning about other countries, but she was never taken anywhere, not even when her parents travelled to all kinds of places all over the world. No, she had to stay and get her education she was told, when she pleaded with them to take her along for an adventure. She had obligations. There was going to be a day when she would be able to travel and see the world as well, just not now. Education was more important.

So Josephine had to just dream about all of those exotic foreign places for now, but one day she was going to see them all. No one was ever going to stop her from doing that. Not even her absent parents, who only spent time with her when they quizzed her on her knowledge and what she had learned in school so far. They never even ate together, since Josephine was supposed to eat with her governess and was only supposed to see her parents when she entered their chambers every evening at seven forty-five to say goodnight. If she was lucky, her mother would come and listen in during her lessons every now and then, and she would get to hug her afterwards, even if it was only a short hug.

Once they took her with them to a gallery opening where they were invited as guests of honor. Josephine had enjoyed that immensely. Especially when all the photographers were yelling and taking pictures and asking her to smile for them. That was a lot of fun. But it had only happened that one time. She was hoping for more.

"So, tell me, Josephine," Ms. Camilla said. "How many people live in London, the capital of England?"

Josephine sighed. "Do I have to? I want to just enjoy the sound of the waves and the fresh air."

"Yes, I know. But learning is important, too. You know that."

Josephine sighed again and looked up at her governess. How she loathed the woman. She was the person closest to her, but sometimes Josephine wondered if she was even human at all. Sometimes she would imagine her being a robot that her parents had bought to mind her. Josephine would picture her in her chambers putting in new batteries or charging herself up by plugging into the wall outlet. That always made Josephine laugh.

"So? I know you know this one, Josephine. I'm taking it easy on you now."

"Twelve million people," she answered. "Making it the largest city in Europe. The country of England is one of the world's most famous and wealthiest. The country is seventy-four times smaller than the United States. The people of England consume more tea per capita than in any other country in the world. Most police officers in England do not carry guns with them unless it is an extreme emergency. The oldest zoo in the world opened in England, in the city of London, in 1828. In Medieval England, beer was a common breakfast beverage. Shoelaces were invented in England in 1790. England is home to the famous rock and roll band *The Beatles*, as well as *The Rolling Stones, Pink Floyd,* and many other rock bands."

Josephine breathed and looked up at Ms. Camilla, waiting for her reaction. Ms. Camilla nodded with tight lips. "Very well then. If you insist on making fun of me, then maybe I should talk to your parents."

Josephine stopped smiling. She shook her head. "Sorry," she said.

"Maybe it was a mistake to come out here. Let's get back and finish our work," Ms. Camilla said.

Josephine felt the tears pressing. She really wanted to go down to the beach first. She wanted to put her feet in the ocean and feel how cold it was. She wanted to breathe the salty air for at least a few minutes more, she wanted to run across the sand, even if her dress might get sandy or wet. She just wanted to have a little fun for once.

Is that so hard to understand?

Ms. Camilla grabbed her arm. Josephine pulled it out of her grip. "I don't want to," she said with tears in her voice. She knew she sounded like a small child with her shrill voice, but enough was enough.

"What are you saying? Miss Josephine Gyldenstjerne. You

are to obey whatever I tell you to do. If I say we go back, we go back immediately. It's not up for discussion. Would you rather have your father send you away to boarding school?"

Josephine snorted. Her heart was racing and she didn't know what to do. She only knew that she was determined not to go with the governess back to that boring old house and all the boring books. She stomped her feet like a four-year-old.

"I want to go down to the beach!"

"But we have just been to the beach," Ms. Camilla said.

"I want to go all the way down there. I want to have my feet in the sand. I want to feel the ocean. I want to make a sandcastle!"

"Miss Josephine!" Ms. Camilla was yelling now, dismayed. "Are you raising your voice to me? Because I will not have that. You come here this instant and follow me back to the house. I will have to call up your parents and have them come up with a proper punishment for this behavior. Never have I..." Ms. Camilla put her hand in her pocket and pulled out a cellphone. "I'm calling them now. They should know what is going on. Your father will be very angry. He is at a very important meeting today and has no time to deal with this. And your mother is getting ready to go to Skagen for a couple of days. She has to meet with the jeweler about the earrings she ordered and try on the dress for the Royal wedding next month." She looked at Josephine, who had started to back up. "Come back here, young lady."

Josephine shook her head. "No," she said. "You're gonna call them anyway. I might as well have my fun first." Then she turned around and started descending towards the beach.

"Miss Josephine!" she heard her governess call behind her, but she didn't care one bit. She ran and felt the wind lift her hair and it was almost as if she was flying. She couldn't help laughing and smiling while she ran down the dunes and into the sand, where she felt it tickle her toes in her sandals. Finally, *finally*, she was going to feel the ocean. Finally, she was on her own. Ms. Camilla was probably still yelling, but the wind drowned out her voice, much to Josephine's pleasure. She pulled up her dress to better run faster, something she hadn't been allowed to do for a very long time, except during her tennis lessons with Mr. Henrik. It felt so good that she had to laugh as loudly as she could and scream out her joy.

9

———————

APRIL 2013

The water felt amazing touching Josephine's feet and covering her expensive sandals. She chuckled and looked down as a wave came in and it reached her knees. Even though she had lifted up her dress, it still got wet on the bottom, but she didn't care. Not about the dress, not about her parents, or even about Ms. Camilla, who was probably still yelling at her from the dunes. She didn't even care enough to look back and see if she had followed her or was coming for her. It didn't matter. All that mattered was that Josephine had a few minutes to herself doing exactly what she felt like.

She laughed out loud again and stomped her feet, making the water splash up high. She closed her eyes and danced while soaking her dress and thighs in the ice cold water. When she opened them again, she spotted someone on the beach, someone walking a dog. Josephine looked at where she had come down to the beach and spotted Ms. Camilla still standing up there, probably just waiting for her to come back, since she couldn't walk in the sand with her high heeled shoes and she was too prim and proper to take them off. Josephine waved at her, then ran towards the dog that was playing in the water just like she was.

"Be careful, he's a little playful," the owner said as Josephine approached the dog and it started jumping around her in joy. Josephine laughed and looked at the owner. An old lady wearing a green rain jacket with the hood covering her head.

"Can I pet him?"

Josephine was filled with joy once again as the old lady nodded with a gentle smile. She wasn't allowed to have pets and the only dogs she ever saw were the ones her dad used on his hunts with his friends. They weren't playful and friendly like this one. Josephine laughed when it jumped on her. She touched its ears and face and felt how incredibly soft it was.

"Django," the owner said and walked closer. She grabbed the collar and pulled him down from Josephine. "We don't jump on people. Especially not small girls in very pretty dresses."

"Is that his name?" Josephine asked. "Django?"

The old lady smiled. "That it is. Do you like it?"

"I love it. It's so cute."

The old lady chuckled. "I thought so, too."

"Is it gonna rain soon?" Josephine asked.

The old lady looked confused. "I don't think so. The weatherman on TV this morning said sunshine all day."

"Why are you wearing a rain jacket, then?"

The old lady chuckled. "Oh, that." She leaned over and looked into Josephine's eyes. Josephine liked her eyes, they were nice and friendly. "That is just for fun."

Josephine laughed. "That's funny."

Django started licking her hand and Josephine chuckled. Oh how she had always wanted a dog like this one, a friend to keep her company during the long days, a friend she could walk with outside in the yard or at the beach like the old lady. She looked at the woman in the thick raincoat and suddenly spotted something sticking out from inside of the coat.

"What's that?" she said.

"This thing?" the lady asked and pulled out the most beautiful old doll that Josephine had ever seen. She showed it to Josephine.

"Yes, that. Is it yours?"

The old lady nodded. "That's my dolly. Do you like her?"

Josephine nodded eagerly. Like any other six-year-old girl, she could never get enough of dolls. "I love it. Does it have a name?"

The old lady nodded with a big smile. "It does. Her name is Little Miss Jasmine. Do you want to try and hold her?"

Django was running around playfully in the water still as Josephine was handed the doll. She looked at it with stars in her eyes. "She is so beautiful."

"It's an old doll. My daughter used to play with it. The one eye is broken, but she is still pretty, I think."

"Your daughter is very lucky."

The old lady tilted her head and looked at Josephine. "I have more at my house. Would you like to see them?"

10

———————

APRIL 2013

"What a beautiful day, huh?" said Hanne, the producer. She was standing next to Patrick on the top deck of the small ferry. Patrick looked at the island approaching in the distance through his dark sunglasses. He smoked his cigarette and blew out smoke that the wind instantly carried away.

"So are you ready to take in a new town?" she continued. "We've never been to Fanoe before. They are really excited about us coming. The newspaper has been writing about it for weeks and the local TV-station has been talking non-stop about it as well. It's a big thing for a small community like this. It gives a lot of great publicity for the show and you know how important that is. So, put on your famous smile and give them a fantastic show, alright?"

Patrick scoffed and smoked again. He hated these so-called pep talks that Hanne always wanted to have before entering a new city. Like this was going to be any different than the rest, just because it was a small island in the middle of nowhere. It was all the same. Little did Hanne know that for Patrick this was actually going to be very different than all the other places they had been. He had something special planned, something that would bring him much joy.

"You're not hung-over again, are you?" she asked and tried to look into his eyes through the glasses. "I need you at your best."

"I'm fine," he grumbled. He wasn't hungover. He was still riding the rush of last night's kill, but the buzz had started to wear off. He hadn't been able to sleep once he got back to the hotel room. The adrenalin had been rushing through his veins, so instead he had taken the car and driven around the town for hours, racing every car he could see on the road.

"Good. 'Cause you are our guy, you know that. Without you, there would—"

"...be no show, I know," Patrick said. "I'm just saving my energy for later. You know, to give them what they came for."

Hanne patted Patrick on the back with a smile. He considered grabbing her and throwing her off the boat. They were alone on the top deck. No one would ever know. He could say that she fell by accident because she was leaning over the edge to look at the water. Patrick felt the rush of adrenalin again. Ah, that wonderful sensation of being alive that he loved so much. He had been so angry all morning, after skimming through the morning paper at the hotel and realizing that there was nothing in it about the body of the Asian girl that he had placed in the restroom at the rest area, sitting on the toilet. He had even left his signature mark on her body. But it hadn't had the effect he wanted it to. At least not yet. Patrick liked reading about his own killings. He especially liked to read about how the police still had no clue who he was. Hell, they didn't even know how many he had killed so far. Only about half of them had been in the papers anyway. That's why he started to leave the mark. To make them see the connection. He wanted them to know what he was capable of. How powerful he was.

He smiled mischievously and looked at the small woman next to him. The water was splashing underneath the ferry. It was still freezing cold at this time of year. She would die very quickly after she hit the water. Now Patrick was chuckling and Hanne noticed.

She smiled. "It's good to see you happy again. For a moment there I was afraid you were getting burnt out or something. It's important to take good care of our host, believe me I know all about that. I have learned my lesson. Can't repeat what happened to Rikke Bo when she was the host of *Dancing Stars*. I worked on the show back then, when she lost it, and that was not fun."

Patrick laughed, but not because of what Hanne had told him. He laughed because he imagined Hanne's facial expression on her way down towards the water. He tried to imagine what would go through her pathetic mind in those terrifying last moments when she knew she was going to die and she knew who had thrown her. Would she feel regret for being so cold-hearted? Would she think of her children that she was always away from? Or would she maybe regret having spent so many hours doing ridiculous TV shows that no one cared about and that were forgotten as fast as they became a success? Maybe not. Maybe she would just think: *You freaking bastard!*

That's what he hoped.

"That's my boy," she said and patted him on his shoulder again. "Smiling and laughing again. That's what I like to see. Those shiny white teeth. Keep it up, Patrick. They're hungry for you on that island. They are desperate for that smile of yours."

Patrick put his arm around her shoulder and felt how she was relaxed by his gesture, probably thinking that he liked her. He tightened his grip slightly and felt her get uneasy. This was it. This was when the anxiousness hit, when the victim first started suspecting that something was wrong, but still refused to believe it.

"Wow you have strong arms," she said with a slight shiver to her voice. Patrick adored the sound of that shiver. It was what fed him.

"I work out," he said and tightened it some more. All it would take would be one quick movement and she would be flying. She was so tiny, so light, it was going to be a piece of cake.

"I feel that. You're kind of hurting me a little," she said.

That's the point!

A door opened behind them. A cameraman Patrick didn't remember the name of came out to them. "Hey guys, they need you downstairs."

Patrick sighed deeply and loosened his grip. The moment had passed. Hanne pulled his arm away and started walking towards the door leading to the stairs. She opened the heavy iron door and looked at him.

"Are you coming?"

11

———————

JULY 1997

The trip in the ice cream truck was very long and Nina couldn't even look out of the windows, since there were none. And, most unfortunately, there was no ice cream either. None that she could see. So Nina started knocking on the door she had come in through.

"Hello? Ice cream lady? I think I'm locked in the car."

But no one answered. The car was still moving and it was very dark. Nina never liked the dark much and her mother always left a small nightlight on so she wouldn't be scared. But she was scared now, really scared. She didn't even want ice cream anymore. She wanted to go back to the playground, back to her mother, back to where she would be safe.

"Hello? Could someone please help me out?" she tried again, but still no answer. Now Nina felt like crying. This wasn't fun anymore. And it was her own fault for disobeying her mother, for not doing as she was told. Nina curled up in a corner and started crying. Carefully, she folded her hands and started praying.

"Please God, please help me get out of this. Help me get back home. I promise I will always do as I'm told from now on. I'll never complain about having to wear dresses again. I promise. I really do, God."

Nina wiped her tears away as she felt the vehicle come to a stop. There were voices outside, then finally someone seemed to be touching the door.

That's it. God heard me. I'm going home now.

The door slid open and the ice cream lady's face appeared. Nina smiled, relieved, but then realized the woman wasn't alone. There was a man with her and he didn't have nice eyes. He was holding something in his hands. A white cloth that, as he stepped forward, he pressed against Nina's mouth and nose, so she could hardly breathe. She tried to scream, but nothing but muffled sounds came out. She tried to move, but suddenly she felt so tired she could hardly lift her arms. Dizziness came over her and everything started spinning. She couldn't even hold her eyes open, and soon she was flying in a sea of stars.

When she woke up hours later, she was in a flat. She was lying on a bed. When she opened her eyes, the ice cream lady came to her and handed her a piece of bread and some water in a bottle. Nina drank and ate greedily. Then the lady followed her to the bathroom and back to the bed again afterwards. She didn't look as nice as she had when she'd offered Nina the ice cream. No, she seemed angry, or upset or something.

"Where am I?" Nina asked, when she lay down on the bed again. The mattress was green and had yellow spots on it.

The ice cream lady didn't answer; she kept looking at Nina, like she was examining her. Then she asked her to open her mouth and she held on to her chin way too hard, while looking at her teeth. The lady then grabbed her dress and pulled it up. Nina whimpered. She didn't like it, but the lady continued anyway. She grabbed her panties and pulled them down, then examined her privates. Afterwards, she walked away. Nina pulled her panties back on while sobbing and watched as the lady talked to the man at the other end of the room. They had a short conversation while the man's eyes were fixed on Nina. He handed the lady what appeared to be a roll of money. Uncomfortable with the man's glare, Nina looked down at the floor while sitting on the edge of the bed. Soon the lady came back. She sat down next to Nina.

"I bet you're wondering why you're here," she said.

Nina nodded while pressing back tears.

"Well, your mother no longer wants you. She told us to take you away." The woman paused and looked at Nina. Then she shook her head. "What did you do, huh? Have you been acting very bad lately?"

Now Nina couldn't hold back the tears any longer. She couldn't believe it. Her own mother didn't want her?

"Don't feel sorry for yourself," the lady said. "You did this. You put this upon yourself. If only you had listened to your mother more, then she wouldn't have sent you away, now would she? I guess you're just too much for her to handle, so now we have found someone else who will take good care of you. But you must promise me to behave. You must promise me to do everything this nice man tells you to. His name is Sergei. He will take you to a new home where he has work for you to do. If you do it nicely and to his satisfaction, he will take good care of you, okay?"

Nina sniffled and looked at the man with the almost black eyes. He looked dirty and sweaty. His hair was glistening. How could her mother have sent her away to be with a man, when they both hated men so much? Was that her punishment for her? Had she really been that bad?

"We leave in a few seconds," he said. His Danish was poor and hard for her to understand.

"Where are we going?" Nina asked, while wiping away her tears.

The man smiled. Some of his teeth were brown and Nina wondered if that was because he hadn't brushed them well enough like her mother always told her to.

"Don't you worry about that," the lady said and helped Nina get up. "Just behave and everything will be fine."

"Come on," Sergei said in horribly bad Danish. "The car is waiting outside."

12

APRIL 2013

On Wednesday at around noon I usually had lunch with my neighbor from across the street, Sophia. She was a teacher at the local school, but was on maternity leave now with her newborn. Today I had prepared a nice salmon quiche with spinach and feta cheese. It was one of my favorite dishes to make.

Sophia came over just before noon and sat in my kitchen while her baby was sleeping in the carriage. Like most Danish moms, she had left the carriage outside on the porch so the baby could sleep in the fresh air, as the doctors recommended. That always made them sleep better and longer, and it was good for their lungs and the whole respiratory system. Her baby was a heavy sleeper, so usually we would have two hours to chat, something we both needed a lot. With her six kids and no husband, she needed to unburden herself every now and then, and so did I, especially today, since I had just found out the day before that my dad had a girlfriend.

"I can't believe he never told you about her," Sophia said, while I cut a piece of the quiche and put it on her plate. "I mean, how long have they been going out?"

"He said they had known each other for two months."

"Two months?"

I nodded and poured some water in our glasses.

"I don't believe it," Sophia continued. "I mean, you'd think we would have known, right? This is a small island. Someone must have seen them together. Why haven't we heard anything?"

"My guess is they have kept mostly to themselves. Maybe because my dad was afraid I'd get upset." I put some quiche on my fork and put it in my mouth. It wasn't the greatest quiche I'd made, but it would do.

"I'm loving this, by the way," Sophia said with her mouth full, pointing at the food on her plate with her fork. "It's really good. I tell you, if you didn't cook for me every Wednesday like you do, I wouldn't get anything proper to eat all week. I don't have the time or the energy to cook. I mean, I do spaghetti and meat sauce and lasagna now and then, but nothing like this."

I was flattered. I had never been much of a cook, but the last couple of months I had been practicing a lot, much to my children's surprise and delight. They loved my food and that made me feel really good. I had discovered that I liked pleasing others with good food. And for some strange reason, I enjoyed watching them eat it. Maybe it was because my mother had never cooked much and I was always so jealous of my classmates who came home to freshly baked buns or cake, and all I ever had after school was cereal that I poured into a bowl myself. I wanted to be different than my mother, so I had started baking a lot lately, and then I ate what I'd made with my kids and sometimes my dad, in the afternoon once they got back from school. It wasn't good for my weight, but the kids seemed to love getting a break like that with me, especially Maya, who was always on the run these days. It was good for her to have that break every now and then, and in that way I got to talk to her as well. Victor was different. He just ate while staring at the table saying close to nothing, before he stormed out to the yard to play with his precious trees.

"Well, I'm glad you like it," I answered, and ate another bite. I looked at the puffed dough on the corner of the kitchen table. I was going to make it into small buns for this afternoon as soon as we were done eating. Maybe I'd put some egg and sugar on top to make it a little sweeter. "So are your kids ready for the audition this Saturday?" I asked before sipping my water.

Sophia nodded. "Ida is singing all day, so is Christoffer. And it's the same songs over and over again. I'm going nuts, I can't get them out of my head." Sophia chuckled, then kept on eating. "You're still going with me, right?"

"Sure. I want to see what it's like."

"Good. 'Cause I need you to take care of the three young ones while Christoffer and Ida audition. I can have the baby in a sling on my chest, but the other ones, I don't know."

"What if we ask Maya to take care of them at home, in your house?" I asked, hoping to get out of babysitting myself. "I'll pay her what she wants. You don't have to worry about that."

Sophia's face lit up. "That would be great. I'm really looking forward to going, and it would be rough with all those kids, you know?"

"I know," I said and got up. "I'm sure she won't mind. Do you want some coffee?"

"Yes, please. That would be great. I never have time to make real coffee anymore. I use that instant crap and it really tastes like water. I need my coffee good and strong."

I smiled and poured water in the pot. "I'll make it so strong you won't sleep for days," I said. Suddenly our conversation was interrupted by the sound of sirens.

Sophia got up from her chair. We both walked to the window. Far away, we could see the island's only police car driving towards the beach. It was very rare that the police car actually had to put on its siren, so naturally we were curious.

"What's going on?" Sophia wondered aloud.

13

APRIL 2013

We put on our jackets, took the baby-carriage, and walked down to the beach, following the sound of the siren and the blue light in the distance. When we got down there, we spotted all of the island's six police officers running around like they were searching for something. On a dune in the distance, we spotted a woman talking to one of the officers. She was sitting on a stretcher belonging to an ambulance parked right next to her. Sophia and I looked at each other, then decided—without speaking a word—that we had to get closer to figure out what was going on. Luckily, one of the officers, Morten Bredballe, came towards us just as we started descending towards the beach area. Sophia knew him, since he had often helped her contacting the fathers of a few of her children that still lived on the island, when they didn't pay their child support.

"What's going on here?" she asked.

Officer Morten looked at her, perplexed. "A child is missing. A little girl."

I gasped, thinking about Helle's story. "Could she have drowned?" I asked.

The officer sighed. "That's what I would have usually thought, but this is different."

"Why is it different?" I asked.

"Well, the woman you see over there is the girl's governess. She was down here with her when she disappeared. She saw her talk to someone, then walk off with that person willingly. The woman tried to run after them and stop them, but fell and hurt her leg. She couldn't get up on her own."

"So, she saw who it was?" Sophia asked. "Can't you just find that person then?"

"She didn't see their face. She doesn't even know if it's a man or a woman. All she saw was someone with a dog, dressed in a heavy raincoat, walk up to the child and talk to her. Then the girl took the person's hand and they walked off. Disappeared between the dunes over there," Officer Morten said, and pointed to our right. A small trail went up through the dunes and into the grass. The place was packed with summer cabins behind it. "Do you think the girl might be in one of the cabins?" I asked.

"That's where we're going to look now. Knock on every door there is," he said with a deep sigh. "I hate when it's kids, you know?"

I nodded. That had to be the worst part of the job as a policeman, when it was an incident that involved children. "Who wears a raincoat when the sun is shining?" I asked.

The officer shrugged. "That's what I'd like to know. The

governess first thought it was harmless for the girl to talk to the person and pet the dog, and that she would eventually come back. So at first she didn't do anything. Plus, she was on the phone with the kid's father. Well, it's all a mess right now. All I want is to find the girl before this evolves into a bigger problem. It might just be some deranged old man or woman, maybe even someone senile who thinks it was his or her daughter or something. Maybe they offered her some candy. Hopefully, whoever it is will let her go back home soon."

"We'll keep an eye out for her as well," I said. "What's her name?"

"Her name is Josephine Gyldenstjerne. They're visitors to the island, but come here every year."

I looked at the officer. "Gyldenstjerne? As in the Count and Countess Gyldenstjerne? Is she their daughter?"

Officer Morten sighed again. "Yes, she is. That's why we're a little nervous that this isn't a coincidence. This might be a kidnapping for ransom."

"I see."

"How old is she?" Sophia asked. "We need to know what we're looking for in case we do see something."

"She's six years old. Has long blonde hair and blue eyes. Slightly chubby. She's wearing a white dress. That's all I know. Now if you'll excuse me, I have to go."

"Of course, Officer. We'll keep an eye out for her," I said and let him walk past us.

As Sophia and I walked back towards our own neighborhood, I couldn't help but think that Helle's daughter had also been six years old when she disappeared.

14

———————

APRIL 2013

Josephine walked inside the old lady's house and followed her into the living room. She had stopped thinking about Ms. Camilla and her parents. All that was in her head was the spectacular doll, and she really wanted to see all of them. Ms. Camilla had to wait. Josephine knew she would be in trouble for this, but she was already in deep trouble for running down to the beach when Ms. Camilla had told her not to, so what did it matter?

Django was playing around, and Josephine patted his back. As she followed the nice old lady into the living room, she paused and gasped. In there, on shelves from wall to wall, in every chair and on every couch, were dolls. Hundreds, maybe even thousands of them. Dolls in all sizes and all with different faces. Josephine, who had always loved dolls more than anything in the whole wide world, shrieked with joy.

"You like them?" the old woman asked with a smile.

Josephine nodded eagerly. "They're beautiful."

"I make them myself," the lady said.

Josephine walked closer to one sitting on the couch. She reached out her hand, trying to touch its leg.

"You can look, but don't touch them," the lady said behind her. "They're very delicate. I don't want them to get greasy and dirty. They are to be looked at, not touched, understand?"

Josephine nodded, even though she didn't understand. Why would anyone have that many dolls and never play with them? It seemed silly. If they were hers, she would play with them every day. Except Ms. Camilla would never let her. Josephine growled at the thought of going back to the mansion. But eventually she would have to. There was no way out.

"How do you even make them?" Josephine asked, while studying the doll in front of her. It had blonde hair just like her and looked so lifelike. It was big, too. Almost as big as her.

"Oh, it's really difficult. Took me many years to learn. Do you want to see where I make them?" the lady asked with a gentle voice.

Josephine nodded. "Yes, please. I would be delighted to."

"What great manners, you have. Your parents must have raised you well," the lady remarked, and started walking towards a closed door. When she opened it, a set of stairs leading down appeared. "It's in the basement," she said and signaled for Josephine to follow her.

The basement was deep and it got colder the further they walked down. Josephine was freezing because she was still wet from being in the water, and she rubbed her arms to generate some warmth. Soon a big room opened up. It had low ceilings, but the lady could still stand upright. A big desk was leaning against the wall. The lady turned on the lamp and Josephine spotted a lot of tools that she knew about from her books. One of them was a scalpel. Josephine had read about doctors using them. There was also a pair of rubber gloves, scissors, a whole box of needles, lots of string, tweezers, then a bottle of something called Borax; she didn't know what that was for. Next to the table were four big bags of something else Josephine didn't recognize.

"That's excelsior," the lady said when she saw Josephine looking at them. "I use that to fill out their bodies."

"And what is that?" Josephine asked and pointed.

"That, my dear, is a box of fake eyes." The lady shook the box and laughed.

Josephine thought they looked a little creepy. All those small eyes staring at her. "So this is where you make the dolls?" she asked, and looked around in the room. A big lifelike doll was standing in one corner looking back at her.

"Yes, it is. Do you like it here?"

Josephine shrugged. She spotted something in the other corner. It looked like the cages where her daddy kept his big dogs that he used for hunting.

"What do you use that for?" she asked.

The old lady smiled widely. "That, my dear, is for you."

15

___

APRIL 2013

"**I** love you, Fanoe!"

Patrick was poking out from the car's sunroof and stood with his arms stretched above his head, still wearing sunglasses, while the car slowly moved from the ferry's deck onto the quay. He had been angry with the producers for not renting a convertible for him to arrive in, so everybody could see him, until he came up with the idea to open the sunroof of the Toyota. A huge crowd had gathered in the parking lot where the ferry docked, and cameras started flashing as soon as he showed his face.

"We love you too, Patrick!" someone from the crowd yelled.

The car moved slowly while fans were screaming out his name and running next to it as it moved. Patrick leaned down and touched hands with several of them. As soon as they were close enough, the journalists started yelling.

"What are you hoping to find here on Fanoe, Patrick?"

Patrick grinned and took off his sunglasses. The girls in the crowd squealed with joy. Patrick winked at the female journalist.

"Love," he said with a deep voice. "I hope to find faith, hope, and love...and some great talent of course!" Then he winked again and put the sunglasses back on with a wide smile. He put his arms up in the air and yelled into the crowd:

"What do you say, Fanoe? Do we have some real Shooting Stars here on the island?"

The crowd went wild. The loud screaming drowned out everything. Patrick laughed. It was like that everywhere he went —and he loved it.

The car moved slowly through the crowd and Patrick managed to touch hands, blow kisses, and even sign autographs on arms and in books. His producer handed him a stack of signed pictures that he threw out among the teenagers, who grabbed them and held them to their chests like prized possessions.

"Had enough yet?" Hanne asked from the driver's seat.

Patrick bent down, sighed, and looked at the huge crowd through the front window of the car. "Not yet," he said. "They really love me."

"Must be great," Hanne said, emotionless, while looking at her fingers.

Patrick heard the crowd start to chant his name to make him poke his head out of the car again.

"Patrick, Patrick, Patrick."

He giggled inside the car while waiting for the right moment. It was all about timing. Making them want more, keeping them thirsty.

"Patrick, Patrick, Patrick!"

Once the chanting reached a crescendo, he knew they were almost ready. They were craving him now.

"Patrick, Patrick, Patrick!"

Almost there. They were almost at the point of giving up, thinking he wasn't going to come back up.

"Patrick, Patrick, Patrick!" they chanted even louder.

Patrick waited just a second longer, then put his arm up through the sunroof and gave them all the finger. The crowd went wild. The screaming wouldn't stop. Patrick laughed. It worked every time. It was his famous signature move. Originally from when the press was always following him around in the beginning, when he had just started doing the show, snooping in his private life, speculating that he might be gay (which they still wrote, but Patrick had stopped caring about).

Running from the paparazzi didn't help—he learned that lesson soon enough—but just standing there, giving them the finger, gave them a picture they could sell and then they would leave him alone. So, in the beginning, all the magazines and papers were filled with Patrick giving the entire world the finger. His producers had told him it was a bad idea, that the public wasn't going to like it, that he was destroying the image of the show. But they were wrong. The people proved them wrong. Screaming teenagers soon showed up to the auditions showing the finger to every camera. It was the youths' rebellion against the boring lives their parents had created for them. These kids wanted more. They wanted to make more of themselves. They wanted to be stars. They all wanted what Patrick had. They wanted to be famous enough to give the world the finger once and for all—*and get away with it.*

16

JULY 1997

It was hard for Nina to keep her tears back as she followed Sergei to the car parked outside the apartment building. It was daytime outside, but the clouds were heavy and grey. It was cold, too. Nina was freezing in her summer dress.

The car was small and he put her in the back seat. Sergei started the engine and they drove off. Nina stared out the window and didn't say a word for hours. She looked at the strange houses that looked nothing like they did on the island. That was when she realized that she had to have been taken away from the island. Her mother had taught her many things, and one of them was to read, so she could read most road signs at home, but these seemed to be different. She didn't quite recognize the words. Was she even in Denmark anymore? Nothing looked the way she was used to. Even the houses were different. They were old and very dirty. Could her mother really have wanted her to go to a dirty place like this? Her mother, the woman who hated when she got dirty.

Nina looked down and realized her dress was no longer pretty. It was dirty, too, and had brown spots on it. Her mommy would be really mad when she saw it. *If* she ever saw it again. Nina looked up and out the window again.

Mommy, where are you? Why have you sent me away like this? Was I really that bad? Please forgive me and let me come home. I promise to never be bad again. I'll never complain about the dresses again. I'll never talk to other kids on the playground again. I promise, Mommy. I promise!

They drove for a long time more, then there was suddenly a sign she could read. It said *Polish Border 50 km.* Nina swallowed hard and felt a slight panic rise. Polish border? She didn't know what it meant but it sounded really far away from Denmark. Far away from her mother. Nina's mother had taught her about the different countries and she had looked at maps before. She knew Poland wasn't a place in Denmark. It was far away. Now the tears started rolling down her cheeks. The uncertainty felt horrible. Was she ever going back? Was she ever going to see her mommy again?

The car came to a sudden halt. It seemed to Nina like they were in the middle of nowhere. She could see a pair of head-lights approach from the other direction. The car stopped across the road. Sergei told her to sit still and then went outside. He talked to some other guy who had come out of the other car, then walked back to the car and opened Nina's door.

"Come on," he said. "Get out of the car. You're going with this guy now."

Nina started shivering. "But...I don't know him...Mommy always said don't go with strangers and..."

"Who cares about Mommy? Get out," Sergei yelled, then grabbed her leg and pulled her out of the car.

Nina hit her head on the ground and scraped her arms. It hurt and she started to cry. Sergei pulled her across the road by her leg, while she was screamed and yelled. Then she heard him speak in a foreign language to the other guy and she felt more hands on her legs, and now she was lifted up and thrown into the other car, where she landed on the back seat.

"Remember to be good," Sergei said as the door closed.

The other man got in and started the engine. Nina thought he looked just like Sergei, but fatter and even dirtier. He was wearing a black leather jacket that squeaked when he turned in his seat to look at Nina.

"I'm Stefan," he said and grinned. His Danish was even worse than Sergei's. "I take good care of you now."

Then they drove off. As Nina peered out the back window with a gasp, she saw Sergei standing back on the road with a big smile and a roll of money in his hands.

17

APRIL 2013

Victor came home from school an hour after Sophia had left me. I couldn't quite let go of the uneasy feeling inside of me after hearing about the missing girl.

"Hi, sweetie," I said, and greeted him in the hallway.

Victor never cared much for being touched, but I really felt like hugging him and holding him tight. It took all my strength not to.

"How was your day?"

Victor stormed past me without answering, without even looking at me. That was just the way he was. I wouldn't say I was getting used to it, because I don't think you ever get used to not having your child respond to you, but I was beginning to accept the fact that it was part of his personality. His lack of social skills was just a part of him. It made me appreciate it even more when he did talk to me.

"I have baked buns," I said, and followed him into the kitchen where he sat down, still without looking at me. Knowing he liked things to be like they always were, I had already prepared a plate for him that I now placed in front of him. He started eating without a word. I grabbed my coffee and sat down in front of him. Since we moved to the island, his condition had gotten slightly better, but there were still days when I wouldn't get a word out of him. I was working closely with his teachers and they had been very helpful through it all. But I still got the sense that he was only really happy when he was out in the yard playing with the trees. That was all he ever wanted to do, so I let him.

"So, are the kids in school talking about the TV show? I heard the host, that Patrick guy, is coming to the island today. They said on the radio that he's down at the quay right now, causing a traffic jam, and the ferry is going to be late going back to Esbjerg."

Victor didn't answer, but I knew he heard me. I knew he hated small talk and he didn't feel obligated to answer if I didn't say anything important. I continued anyway.

"Do you think they'll find this year's winner here at Fanoe Island, huh?" I sipped my coffee while Victor ate. "Maybe one of Sophia's kids will win, huh? Wouldn't that be great? Maybe Ida?"

Victor stopped chewing. I couldn't help smiling. I knew he had grown very fond of Ida. She was a year younger than him, only six years old, but she was very pretty with her long blonde hair and she was extremely sweet. "Would you like that, Victor? Would you like for her to win and become famous?"

He didn't answer. I laughed on the inside. It felt good to know that he was capable of that kind of emotion. I wanted him to like her and was planning on asking Sophia to bring her over more often. It was good for him to be with other children.

Victor finished his raspberry juice and swallowed the last bite of his bun. Then it was like he froze.

"Victor, are you all right?" I asked after a little while when he hadn't moved at all.

Suddenly, he lifted his head and stared directly into my eyes. I couldn't help but smile, since it was so seldom lately that I got to see his eyes and feel the close connection between us that we used to have. But then it happened, the thing I hated the most in the entire world. Victor's eyes rolled back in his head and he started shaking. I jumped up from my chair, knocking over my cup and spilling hot coffee all over the table. I grabbed Victor and held him in my arms while his body spasmed.

"Oh, no, not this," I yelled. "Please, make it go away. Please, make it stop."

It had been six months at least since his last seizure and I had hoped it was over, that he had finally outgrown them like his doctor used to say he would one day. I stroked his hair and kissed his forehead while his body was shaking between my arms. The doctors had told me to always hold him so he wouldn't hurt himself.

"It's okay, Victor. I've got you. Don't worry," I said with an anxious heart. I hated these seizures. I hated everything about them. Mostly I hated how helpless I was when they occurred.

Please don't let him swallow his tongue. Please make this stop.

Victor said something. A mumbling emerged from his mouth. "What are you saying, Victor? Are you trying to tell me something?" I bent down to better hear what it was. It was hard to make anything out of it. It sounded like he'd said *baby doll*.

18

———————

APRIL 2013

Victor's seizure stopped just as suddenly as it had started. His body loosened up in my arms and he stopped shaking. Victor opened his eyes and looked at me. I breathed in a sigh of relief.

"Are you okay, Vic?"

He nodded.

"You were out for a moment there, buddy. Did you dream anything? Did you see anything? It was like you tried to speak or something. Were you trying to tell me something?"

Victor looked down.

"You can tell me. I won't get mad."

Victor opened his mouth and spoke very softly: "Dolls. I saw a lot of dolls. Hundreds, maybe even thousands of them."

"Dolls. Okay. That makes sense. What else? Did you see anything else?" I asked.

Victor lifted his head once again and looked at me. "A bowtie. Look out for the bowtie," he said.

"Bowtie, okay."

Victor took one last look at me, then walked fast with his head bowed through the living room and out into the yard. I sighed and followed him with my eyes. If only I knew what went on inside of that boy's head. Sometimes it seemed like he was carrying the entire world on his shoulders. It scared me a little, to be honest. It was too much for such a young boy to deal with. At his age, he was supposed to have fun and play around. The rest of his life was going to contain plenty of serious stuff, especially with his condition. There weren't many workplaces around where there was room for someone like Victor.

Seeing him smile and run around in the yard like a normal boy again made my unease settle for a little while, and I went back into the kitchen to get ready for Maya's return from school. I couldn't help but think about the bowtie and wonder what that meant. Did the girl who'd disappeared wear a bowtie? I knew Victor had these senses that no one else had; he had proven that to me more than once. It was like he sometimes knew more than the rest of the world. And from experience, I also knew how important it was to take the things he said very seriously. It wasn't just coincidental rambling. If he saw something or said something like this, it meant I had to remember it. It meant it was important.

"Hi, Mom."

I turned and saw Maya entering the kitchen. She'd just turned fourteen and grew more beautiful with every day that passed. "I baked," I said.

"Yum," she said and sat down. I joined her at the table and had a buttered bun myself.

"So, how was school? You're home a little later than usual."

"Well, a bunch of us went down to the port and saw Patrick arrive on the ferry. It took a while to get back because of all the people."

"You were down there?" I asked, and considered getting angry because she hadn't asked me if it was okay, but then I thought it was alright, she'd been with friends and a whole crowd of people. I had taught myself to pick my battles carefully lately to avoid being the kind of mother who was angry constantly no matter what you told her.

"Yes. I hope it was okay that I went. It was kind of spontaneous. We were actually on our way home on our bikes, when someone told us that Patrick was about to get off the ferry. I couldn't resist seeing it."

"I understand. I guess I would have done the same. Was he as spectacular as they say?" I asked and took another bite. I had put extra sugar on top of the buns to make them sweeter, with great success. It was like eating cake.

"Oh, yes. He is so handsome, Mom, you won't believe it. I think he was even better looking in real life than on TV."

I chuckled when I noticed the glow in my daughter's eyes. "Well, I'm glad you had fun this afternoon."

"Me, too." Maya paused, then looked down at her plate and ate. I sensed she wanted to say something more, but didn't dare. Then she did it anyway. "Could I go down to his hotel tonight after dinner, just for an hour or so? Everybody is hanging out at the front entrance in case he goes out."

I sighed with a smile. I wasn't fond of the idea of my daughter hanging out like a groupie, screaming at him if he showed his face, but it was the kind of thing my own mother never let me do, so a small voice inside of me said to let her do it.

I decided to follow that voice. "Okay—"

My daughter screamed. "Thanks, Mom. You're the best!"

"—on one condition."

My daughter sat still, but was smiling. "Okay? What condition?"

"That you take care of Sophia's younger kids on Saturday when Christoffer and Ida are auditioning."

"But I was planning on going down there too—" she said.

"You can go later, when we're back. It's gonna last all weekend, so you'll also have Sunday. And then there's the sing off on Monday night, where all the contestants perform live at the port. I'll let you go to that as well, if you do this small thing for me on Saturday."

My daughter's eyes grew big and wide. "You've got a deal, Mom."

19

APRIL 2013

Josephine could hardly move around in her aluminum cage; it was even too small for her to stand up straight. All she could do was sit down, and it wasn't long before her legs started to hurt. She tried to move them around, but couldn't even stretch them properly.

When the lady had first grabbed her and thrown her inside of the cage, Josephine had screamed her lungs out. She had tried to break the cage with her hands and kick the door open with her legs, but nothing seemed to work. The lady had left her at first, but was now back, sitting at the desk under the lamp working on something.

"Why are you keeping me in here?" Josephine asked.

But the lady didn't answer. She completely ignored Josephine's pleading and talking. After a while, she gave up on the idea of getting an answer out of her. Instead, she pulled her legs up under her and started rocking back and forth, thinking about how much she suddenly missed Ms. Camilla and the mansion. Hell, she even missed her parents. At this point, Josephine would do anything to get back to her old life and mind numbingly boring routine.

Anything but this.

Every now and then, she would burst into tears and cry like a baby, but not even that would make the lady turn around and look at her. Josephine didn't understand. The lady had seemed so nice. What did she want with her? Why was she keeping her in this cage? Josephine felt so extremely thirsty and she needed to go to the bathroom really badly.

"Excuse me?" she asked, trying to be polite, since the lady had seemed to like that earlier. But the lady still didn't answer. She was sitting by the desk, humming while sewing something, as far as Josephine could see. "Excuse me! I really need to go to the bathroom. I have to pee."

"There is a bucket in your cage. Use that," the lady said without turning around to look at Josephine. "There is also a dog bowl of water to satisfy your thirst." Then she continued her humming and sewing.

Josephine looked at the bucket behind her in the cage. It was an old tin bucket. It was rusty in places. How was she supposed to pee in that? Josephine sobbed loudly as she sat on it. She had to bend her head and back to fit. This was very strange, nothing like anything she had ever done. How long was this going to go on?

Josephine closed her eyes when she finally managed to pee. It felt so good. Such a relief. When she was done, she climbed down from the bucket and sat on the floor of the cage again.

Then she leaned over and drank from the bowl, feeling like a dog. Never had she been so humiliated, she thought, sobbing. The sobbing quickly became crying. This was not good. This wasn't good at all.

But they'll find you. They'll come for you, sure they will. They never even let you go outside alone. They will be looking for you all over.

The thought brought some comfort to her mind and she relaxed a little. This was just for a short period of time. Surely Ms. Camilla had seen the old lady take her with her at the beach and had told the police about her. They would know who she was. The police knew everything, didn't they? Of course they did. They would be here soon. Of course they would. And then the old lady would go to jail for a long time. She was nothing but a crazy old witch...Josephine stopped her train of thought when she had the spooky thought about all the fairy-tales she had read with Ms. Camilla. Some of them had an old lady or an old witch capturing children. Like Hansel and Gretel. An old witch wanting to eat them...Josephine gasped. She cupped her mouth to stop the sound and not draw the old lady's attention. Was that what this old lady was? A witch who was going to eat her? Josephine felt her heart racing in her chest. Like a drum that wouldn't stop beating. She stared at the skinny lady's neck and back and felt a chill run down her own spine. Was that why her parents never let her go out on her own? Were those stories maybe real? Were there real witches in this world who ate small children?

20

APRIL 2013

Patrick was sitting in his hotel room, listening to the cheering and chanting coming from his fans by the front entrance. He was breathing it in, soaking in it, enjoying every second of it.

"So, I say we use this one next time," Hanne said, pointing at a poster of him holding a microphone and screaming out to the audience.

Patrick looked down at it. He didn't care which picture they used for the poster or how they made the trailers for the show. He wasn't into all those kinds of details. He looked good in all of them, that was the important part. Otherwise, he didn't care. Still, the producers insisted he was present at the meetings where those kinds of decisions were made. A few times he had forgotten to go to the meetings and the producers had been angry with him for being absent.

"So, have the meeting in my room, that way you can be sure I'm there," he had answered.

So that's what they did now. All fifteen of the decision makers were now in his hotel room, the top suite, of course, sitting on the couches and chairs, talking every little annoying detail over like it was something he should be interested in. Patrick himself was sitting leaned back in an armchair, swaying his head from side to side, trying to see faces or figures in the ceiling.

"So, we're going with the green spotlight on Patrick again when he enters the stage on Monday, right?" some guy asked.

"No, I think it makes him look sick," Hanne said. "Better to use the yellow."

Patrick rolled his eyes. "That's the point, Hanne. I want to look sick when I enter. I need to be nasty. That's what the teenagers like. They like that I'm not just another pretty boy. I want the green light. It gives me that crazy, lunatic look when I enter."

"I have to agree with Patrick," another producer named Tom said. "The diabolic look is what made Patrick so big; it's what separates him from the other hosts out there. And it fits his nature. He's not just a pretty face like the rest of them. He's a character. He's the maniac inside of us all."

People around the table were nodding. Patrick sighed and leaned back in his chair again to watch the ceiling.

Stupid morons. Amateurs, all of them. If it wasn't for me, they would get nowhere. I'm the show. I'm the character. Without me, they would be out of job.

"Okay," sighed Hanne and wrote something on her notepad.

"We go with the green diabolic light for the entrance again. But please try and control that finger of yours while you're up on stage. We have all seen it now, hell all of Denmark has seen it. It upsets the parents."

"What?" Patrick sat up. He looked at Hanne and took off his sunglasses.

"But, Hanne," Tom said. "The finger is his *thing*. They all come to see him do it. You can't stop him from doing that. That would be stupid."

Hanne sighed again. "I know we've been over this before. But the ratings show that we're losing audience in the 25-35 group, and our focus group polls have shown that the finger has a lot to do with that. The numbers don't lie, Tom."

Patrick got up with a snort. He stared at the small woman. Oh, how he wanted to grab her and snap her neck, right here and now. It would be so easy. Patrick growled and walked to the window. A fan spotted him from the street.

"There he is! Patrick!" she yelled. Others came running and stared at him as well. Patrick put his face to the window, then opened the doors and walked outside on the balcony. The entire street was filled with teenagers. They started screaming when they spotted him. Patrick smiled, then raised his arm and slowly rolled up the finger. The crowd went ballistic.

"See, I told you they want it," he yelled at the producers in the room. "They freaking love it!"

"But those are teenagers, Patrick. This show has viewers other than teenagers," Hanne yelled back. "We need the 25-35 year olds, as well. You alienate a lot of people by raising your finger like that."

"Ah, to hell with them," Patrick mumbled and looked down at the crowd. He felt stirred up inside. Even more than usual. There was something about this island that made him so angry, so out of control. Usually he would never go for the kill until the show was over and they were about to leave town, but maybe, just maybe he was going to bend his rules a little this time. Heaven knows his body craved it. It was like he was in withdrawal, like a drug addict he needed his fix to not go crazy. And he knew exactly how he was going get it.

Patrick laughed manically as he grabbed onto the railing of the balcony and climbed up on it. Then he let go with his hands and stood on the railing without holding on. The crowd went quiet. Then they screamed in joy as Patrick started whining his famous scream that they all loved so much.

That's it, you suckers. Scream all you want. Tonight, I'm the one who's gonna have all the fun.

21

—————

JULY 1997

They had to cross the border on foot, Stefan said. He parked the car in a deserted area and told Nina to get out.

"We walk now," he grunted and started to go.

Nina hesitated.

"Come on," he said and grabbed her arm. "Family is waiting for you on other side, but we have no papers. Once we're over border, you will have new mommy."

Nina started crying again as the sweaty man pulled her arm. She didn't want a new mommy, she already had one. But the man was too strong and she couldn't fight him. He grabbed her around the waist and started carrying her into the darkness. Nina screamed and whimpered, but no one could hear her out there in the middle of nowhere. Once he got tired of carrying her, he put her down on the ground. Then he slapped her across the face.

"You walk now, okay?"

Nina was crying hard now and the man lifted his hand as if to hit her again. Nina stopped crying, then promised him she would walk from now on.

"Cars are waiting on the other side once we get past border," Stefan said, and continued to walk.

Nina followed him, whimpering and crying, but she did as he wanted her to. What else could she do? Every now and then she looked back at the car they had left behind, but soon it was out of sight and there was nothing but darkness surrounding her. They walked all night, crossing narrow mountain roads and desolate wilderness. Nina could hardly move her legs anymore when they finally reached the ridge leading them across the border.

"Now, you run," Stefan said and pointed down into the valley. "Sprint. See those flashlights? They are people waiting for you. You go to them; they take good care of you now."

"Aren't you coming with me?" Nina asked with a shivering voice. She did see the flashlights in the valley, but she had never met those people before.

Stefan grinned. "No. No. I stay here or I go to prison. You belong to them now. No worry, little girl. Good people. Take good care of children. But if you try to run, they will shoot you. Okay?"

Nina's heart was in her throat as she looked down the mountainside at the flashlights flickering in the darkness. Who were those people and why did she have to go with them? Her mother had often told her she would go to boarding school if she didn't behave, to learn manners and respect for authorities. Was this boarding school? Were those people taking her to her new school?

Please, Mommy. I'm scared. I'll be good. I promise. Don't make me go there. Take me home.

Nina felt a push in her back. "You must go, little girl. Before someone finds us. You must go now," Stefan said.

Nina swallowed her tears and looked back one more time before she started running down the mountainside towards the flashlights, towards her new future. The terrain was difficult, and soon Nina tripped over one of the sharp rocks. She cut her leg and was bleeding, then she cried again. She could hear voices in the distance and see the flashlights. Knowing she had to reach the other side before the sun came up (or else she would go to jail, Stefan had told her) she got up once again and started running, even though her leg hurt really bad.

Once Nina reached the valley, she felt exhausted and was bleeding from multiple cuts she'd gotten from rocks and bushes with many thorns. Voices speaking a strange language were coming closer now and three flashlights were pointed at her. The men came closer and now she felt hands on her body, picking her up. She was too tired to look, but felt her body being carried into the back of a van, then the door was closed and she could hear the engine start in the distance.

22

———————

APRIL 2013

Jack came over that evening. He rang the doorbell, and as I opened the door, he handed me a yellow rose.

"It's from my own yard," he said.

I smiled and blushed. I was wearing an old worn out apron and had flour all over my hands and face from the pie I was baking. Jack laughed when he saw it.

"You're busy, I take it?"

"I was just trying out a new pie recipe for dessert. I've been into cooking lately. It's my new hobby. Come on in, you can stay for dinner."

"Are you sure?" Jack said. "I didn't mean to impose or anything. I just saw the rose in the yard earlier and thought you should have it."

I paused and looked at him. "That was really sweet, Jack. Thank you. Come in. My dad is here with his girlfriend, too. The more the merrier, right?"

"That's what I've heard, yes," Jack said and stepped inside. He took off his beanie and showed his thick brown hair. I smiled and put the flower in water. I heard Jack say hello to my dad and Helle in the living room, while I put the pie in the oven and ran upstairs to clean myself up. I put on a little make-up for once and looked at myself in the mirror. It had been awhile since I had done something to look good, and suddenly it felt a little uncomfortable. I wiped off the lipstick to make it more subtle. I had butterflies in my stomach and felt like a young girl all of a sudden. Just because of Jack? Well, I did like him a lot, and I could tell he was comfortable in my presence since he didn't stutter at all anymore while talking to me. And we did have kind of a history together, ever since that night in October when he'd saved me and Victor. I couldn't believe he was actually kind of saving me again tonight. I had been so nervous having my dad's girlfriend over for dinner earlier, but now that Jack was here it was easier. More people to make conversation. That was good for me, because I was horrible at small talk and polite conversation. This was a really good turn of events, I thought to myself.

I ran down the stairs and put the food on the table. I had made lamb and rubbed it with plenty of garlic. With it, I served rosemary roasted potatoes, a Greek salad, and homemade tzatziki. I really hoped they were going to like it. And I really hoped they liked garlic, as there was lots of it.

"Dinner is on the table," I said, as I peeked in the living room where they all sat in front of the fireplace. Victor was on my dad's lap and had put his arms around his neck. I felt a sting of jealousy. Lately, my dad was the only one who got to touch my son and the only one he really talked to. It was always like that with Victor. He picked his favorites and never cared about everybody else or their feelings. It was just not in him to care.

"Where's Maya?" my dad asked, as we sat down around the new heavy oak table in the dining room that I had recently bought with some of the money I made from my bestselling book. I was surprised at how well I was doing and began thinking about writing a new one soon. I just needed that one idea, and so far all that was on my mind was my family and cooking.

"She's out with her friends tonight," I answered and smiled at Helle, who took the chair next to me.

"At this time on a school night?" my dad asked.

"Yes, Dad. At this time on a school night. She and her friends are hanging out down by the Hotel Mellers, you know, the nice one downtown. They're trying to catch a glimpse of Patrick."

Helle chuckled. "Ah, the famous TV host. Yes, everybody in town is talking about him these days."

My dad snorted. "I can't imagine why. I mean, what's the fuss about? I don't get it. He whines like a girl. Why does that get people so excited?"

I shrugged and put a helping of lamb on my plate before I passed it on to Jack on my other side. "Well, he's handsome and he's very funny. You never know what he'll do next. That's what makes him interesting. He's not neat and boring like all the other television hosts. They all look alike. It gets boring. Patrick is different. He puts on a show every time."

Helle nodded. "I'm completely with Emma on this one," she said, and gave me a nice smile.

It felt good to agree with her on this. I was beginning to think I was going to like having her around.

"Patrick is really unique. And the kids love him. The girls go crazy down there. It doesn't all have to be so sleek. It's good that he dares to be himself. It's good for the young to see," she said.

My dad snorted again and poured wine in our glasses. "I still don't get it," he replied. "To me, he's nothing but a freak of nature, a weird faggot."

"Dad!" I looked at him, then at Victor, who luckily seemed to be in a world of his own, hearing nothing of what we were talking about.

"Sorry," my dad said. "But the guy *is* gay, isn't he? I mean, with all the jewelry, the weird clothes? I mean, who wears pink boas if you're a real man, right?"

"Plenty of rock stars, Dad."

Helle nodded. "Steven Tyler for example."

"Thank you, yes. Patrick is a Danish Steven Tyler, just not a rock-star, but close. He expresses himself and he is secure enough in his masculinity to wear those kinds of spectacular clothes. That does not make him gay."

"But do you really want Maya to run around down there and scream at him?" my dad asked with his mouth full. "I mean, what's with the finger and all that? Is that something your kid should think is cool?"

I shrugged. My dad had a point, but I didn't think Maya thought the finger was cool. I just thought she wanted to hang out with her friends and that she found him handsome, that was all. "I don't know," I said. "I think the older generation will never approve of what the younger generation likes. But, I'll admit I don't like the finger part, either. Guess that makes me older, huh?"

Jack chuckled. I gave him a smile. I knew I wasn't going to be able to control everything in my daughter's life any longer, but my dad was right, I probably needed to talk to her about the finger part.

"So, you're a painter, Jack?" Helle asked across the table.

Jack blushed, then nodded. "Wwwell yes. I do ppaint."

"And he's really good at it, too," I added, even though I knew Jack hated to talk about himself. I was trying to make him feel comfortable.

"I need some decorations for the walls in my shop. Maybe I could hire you to paint something for me?" she asked.

"That's a great idea," I said, knowing how badly Jack needed the money. He was taking care of his handicapped sister on a very unstable income. Luckily, she had her disability pension to help out, but he was still always lacking money.

"Could you paint anything that I wanted?" Helle asked.

"Sure," Jack said. "I've done orders before. Wwhat would you like?"

"Well, my shop sells dolls. Souvenirs, as well and trinkets, but mostly dolls and supplies for them, like clothes, headbands and bowties and stuff," she said.

I almost choked on my lamb, thinking about what Victor had said earlier. I started coughing.

"Excuse me," I said, and drank some wine to clear my throat.

"It's mostly the dolls I'm interested in," she continued. "They are my real passion. I love those babies."

"I'll nnneed to come down and see what they lllook like first."

"Sure," she said.

"Maybe I'll go with you," I said. "I'd love see your shop."

23

APRIL 2013

The meeting was over and everyone had finally left Patrick's hotel room. He found the black hoodie in his suitcase and put it on. It still had a couple of bloodstains on the sleeve, but they blended in well with the dark color, he thought. No one would notice.

Patrick then found his black gloves and Balisong, his butterfly knife, and put it inside the pocket of the hoodie. He covered his head and walked out into the hallway. He was alone in the elevator going down. Once in the lobby, he ducked his head and covered his face completely while slipping out through the crowd towards the back exit of the hotel. He was going out on foot this time.

He heard the screaming teenagers outside the front entrance every time the doors were opened and chuckled to himself as he opened the back door and got out without anyone seeing him. He looked back to make sure no one was following him and walked around the corner of the building. He stood at a distance and watched the crowd chanting his name, while looking hopefully at the window of his hotel room. He had left the lights on to make them believe he was still in there. It was the perfect alibi and worked every time. No one suspected him, since he wasn't even able to go out in the streets without being seen and mobbed by fans. It was impossible.

He felt superior in so many ways as he watched his many fans from a distance. They were hollering his name, like he was some freaking god or something. It was amazing. Maybe he was a god, maybe he did have superpowers...It felt like it sometimes. Being able to determine whether or not someone should live. It was the greatest feeling in the world. Nothing would beat it —ever.

Patrick nodded slowly to himself, taking all the cheering and applauding in. This was his, this was him, he had done this, *he* made things happen.

And now he was going to make something else happen. Now he was going to go out and give the people something new to talk about.

Patrick turned his back on the crowd and started walking slowly to stay low, when suddenly two young girls walked towards him on the sidewalk. Patrick bowed his head slightly and put his hands in his pockets, trying to avoid letting them see him. They were giggling and chatting as they walked along. Patrick hated giggling girls most of all. He loathed their happy small lives where nothing bad ever happened. It made his skin crawl and it made him want to make something bad happen to them. Make them feel reality, real life. The brutality of nature.

All these girls lived secure, protected lives, and he hated them for it.

"Is that...?" one of the girls pulled her friend's jacket.

"Do you think...?" the other one said.

They came closer and Patrick gripped the knife in his hand while thinking this was a bad place. Someone would see them there.

"Yes, it is..." the first one said, while bending slightly to see Patrick's face. "It *is* him. It's Patrick!"

Patrick lifted his head and made a sign for them to keep it quiet. They seemed to understand. "Thanks, guys," he said. "I needed a little privacy, you see."

He looked into their faces and saw the excitement in their eyes. They both looked like they could burst.

"Can we have your autograph?" one of them asked.

Patrick smiled and grabbed the pen. He signed her arm. The other girl seemed a little more cautious. Patrick liked that. "Do you want my autograph too, pretty girl?" he asked.

The girl smiled, and before she could answer, Patrick had signed her arm. "Say, you're really beautiful," he said and grabbed her chin. "What's your name?"

She blushed and replied, "Maya."

"Well, hello, Maya," Patrick said smiling. Then he leaned over and whispered in her ear. "I really like you, Maya. I want to get to know you. Meet me Monday night at the show. I'll put your name on the list. Come backstage. But don't tell anyone. " He looked deep into her eyes. Her shy eyes avoided his. "Promise me?" he said and held her hand. Then he kissed it on the top.

"I promise," she answered with the most despicable sweet little voice. Oh, how Patrick loathed everything about pretty little girls. He clenched the knife in his pocket with his other hand and fought the desire to kill her right there.

Then he turned around and made himself disappear between a row of houses.

24

APRIL 2013

Patrick felt like Zorro or maybe Batman in his cape and disguise as he rushed through town to get away from people, to get away from the screaming fans. He didn't run, since that would make him look suspicious, but he speed-walked and avoided people by crossing the street whenever he saw someone. Soon the streets were empty and he was all alone.

Patrick breathed in and enjoyed the silence for a second. Usually, he wasn't very fond of silence, or being alone for that matter, since it always gave him room to think too much, and Patrick did not like to think. He liked to be on the go, always going somewhere, always the center of the action and attention. But when he turned into his alter ego at night and went out to do his thing, then he enjoyed being left alone, then he enjoyed the silence surrounding him.

Because he knew the silence would soon be broken by the sound of him taking yet another life.

Patrick spotted a small light coming from a kiosk on the corner of a building. The sign outside stated that it was open till ten pm. It was five to now.

"Perfect timing," Patrick mumbled, and peeked in through the glass door. A young girl was standing behind the counter, reading a magazine, constantly looking at her watch, probably anxious to go home. She was perfect. No more than fifteen, pretty with long hair.

"Exquisite," Patrick told himself. "Just the way you prefer them: Young, beautiful, and innocent."

He braced himself for what was about to happen next, felt the thrilling rush in his stomach, the chill on his spine. He put his gloved hand on the door handle and opened the door. The small bell above it rang and the girl looked up from her magazine. As her eyes met his, she froze.

"Oh, my God," she exclaimed. She looked down at the cover of her magazine where Patrick's eyes looked back at her. "You're...You're..."

Patrick smiled mischievously. "Indeed, I am."

The girl blushed. "Wow. And you're in *my* shop?"

"So it appears," Patrick answered and walked closer.

"Can I have your autograph?" The girl giggled and Patrick's blood froze at the sound.

Then he pulled out his famous smile. "Well, of course!"

Her eyes became wide and she dove down under the counter to find a notepad. When she lifted her head again, she was holding the pad and a pen. She handed them towards him. "Here. If you could just sign here..."

Patrick grabbed it and pretended he was about to sign it,

when he paused and looked up. "Now, what am I thinking?" he said.

The girl looked at him, confused.

"A pretty girl like you should have a special autograph, shouldn't she?"

The girl's eyes lit up. "A special one?"

"Yes. Of course. All the girls want me to sign their arm or some even on their breasts—those are the NAUGHTY ones."

Patrick had screamed the word out and the girl jumped at the sound. Patrick laughed out loud manically. He loved this moment. "I bet you're feeling just a little bit afraid now, aren't you? Because I yelled like THIS!"

The girl jumped again. Then nodded.

"But, you still refuse to believe that feeling, don't you? You're fighting it inside of you. Because you are, after all, standing in front of a real CELEBRITY, aren't you? And they're not dangerous? They don't mean any harm? They never hurt anyone, especially not a NICE and PRETTY girl like you."

Patrick ended his sentence with his famous smile. The girl stared at him and he could almost hear how her many thoughts were racing through her mind.

"So, now I give you my special autograph, right?"

The girl had backed up and was now standing with her back against the row of cigarettes behind her. "I...I'm not..."

"SURE YOU ARE!" Patrick leaned over the counter. "You want this. You want my autograph on your body." He pulled out his knife. The girl gasped. He walked around the counter and cornered her inside of it, poking the knife at her for fun. Then he ripped her blouse with it and parts of her stomach appeared.

She had nice skin, too. A little pale after a long winter, but nice nonetheless.

"Maybe I should write my name right here. Right there on the skin of your stomach, huh? You think I should leave my autograph there, do you? I could carve the letters in with this knife. Leave you with a memory of me for the rest of your life, huh?"

The girl shook her head. "Please don't—"

"Please don't, please don't," Patrick said, imitating the girl, or any other obnoxious schoolgirl who thought the world was all about her, for that matter.

The girl started crying. Patrick rolled his eyes. "Oh, come on," he said. "Why do all the girls do the same thing? They always cry? Do you really think anyone cares that you start to cry? Huh? Do you?"

The girl was shaking and shook her head. Patrick waved his hand at her in disgust. "And now you're just trying to please me, to say what I want to hear so I won't hurt you, right? That's what everybody does. Well, I've got a news flash for you, baby girl. Try something a little more original for a change. Don't just imitate everybody else, alright? Cause there is a world out there and it'll eat you alive if you're not careful, if you don't learn how to survive. You need to stand out in the crowd. Don't just be mediocre. Don't just be like everybody else."

Now the girl was nodding. Her hands were in front of her face, shaking violently, almost like she was having a seizure. Patrick sighed his annoyance. She was beginning to bore him.

"Please, don't hurt me," she said.

"Please don't hurt me," Patrick repeated with a grimace and while making a girly voice once again.

"What do you want from me? Take the money if you like. I don't care. I only work here."

Patrick smiled again. "Now that's more like it. More feisty, fighting a little for your life. I like that."

"Please, just tell me what you want," she pleaded, crying.

"And now we're back to being boring again. Desperate is boring, sister. Try another approach."

The girl sulked and sobbed. "I don't know what to do."

Patrick laughed and leaned over. "Well, you better come up with something soon, 'cause once I get too bored with you—SNAP—you're dead," he said, and snapped his fingers with the other hand. Then he smiled again. "Isn't this FUN?"

The girl whimpered and covered her face with her hands.

"Ah, now you're doing that. The *I better keep quiet so I don't say anything wrong again and make him mad* approach. Well... It's not quite working for me here. See, I get my kick out of keeping you alive as long as you're worth it, as long as you fight for it. But, if you don't, then I might as well finish you off."

The girl removed her hands and looked at Patrick. Then she picked up a magazine and threw it at him while screaming and yelling at him.

"Like this, huh? You want me to fight like THIS?"

Patrick grabbed the magazine in mid-air, then threw it down on the floor. Then he grinned from ear to ear. "Yes. Exactly like that." Patrick burst into a loud laugh and put the knife back in his pocket. He kept laughing as he pulled backwards away from the girl. He picked up the magazine from the floor, then put it on the pile on the counter. "Nah, I'm just messing with you. Kind of got you there, huh?"

The girl shook her head and slowly her body relaxed. "You... You...you were just kidding? The magazines do always say you like to act crazy..."

Patrick shrugged and walked further away from her, he could sense she came closer. She was right behind him now. He paused and waited till she was close enough.

"...It was just a joke?"

Patrick gave her one more second before he turned around in one swift movement, and pulling out the knife once again, he stabbed her. As she bent over, holding her hands to the blade of the knife, he leaned over and whispered in her ear.

"Yes, sweetie. It's all a joke."

25

———————

APRIL 2013

Just before he left, Jack and I agreed that we would go and see Helle's store the next day. He thanked me for a wonderful dinner, then leaned over and kissed me gently on the cheek. I giggled like a schoolgirl, not because of the kiss, but because of his sweet ways, which reminded me of a young boy's.

My dad and Helle sat in the living room, chatting like an old couple, laughing at each other's comments and just acting like they really enjoyed each other's company. I stood for a little while and watched them, thinking it was great for my dad that he had found someone to share his life with. Then I looked out the window and saw the lights in Jack's house, and started thinking that so could I, if I really wanted it. Jack was a nice guy and I had been waiting for him to ask me out, but so far he hadn't made his move. I didn't know if it was just because he was shy or if he maybe didn't want to. Tonight made me think he was just warming up, but I could be wrong.

Victor suddenly came out to the top of the stairs looking at me. "Victor, sweetie. Why aren't you in bed? I thought you were sound asleep. It's late, buddy, and you have school tomorrow," I said, hurrying up the stairs to him. "Is something wrong? Did you have a bad dream? Are we being too loud?"

Victor seemed to be half asleep when he suddenly spoke. "The bowtie is red, Mommy. The bowtie is red."

"Is that what you came out here to tell me? Did you dream about a bowtie?" I asked, helping him back into his bed. I put the covers over him and sat on the edge of the bed. "It's okay, Victor. It doesn't matter what color the bowtie is. I'll keep an eye out for it. I promise you."

Victor grabbed my arm and held on to it tightly. "No, MOMMY," he yelled. "The bowtie is red because there's blood on it."

His yelling startled me. I felt my heart race faster and faster. What did it mean? Why was he telling me this?

"Go back to sleep now, buddy. We can talk about it in the morning."

Victor seemed to calm down and I left his room after a few minutes of just sitting there and watching him fall asleep. I was worried about him. He kept drifting back and forth between his imaginary world and the real world. I never knew which one he was in or referred to when he told me things like this.

I walked down the stairs and heard my dad and Helle laugh again. I walked in there and sat down to join them, when all of a sudden my cellphone rang. I jumped up and found it on the kitchen table. The display told me it was Maya. My heart started racing again. Had something happened to her?

"Sweetheart?"

Maya was panting on the other end. Something was really wrong. I could hear it even before she spoke. "Mom you need to come now. Something has happened. I need your help."

"What's going on, Maya? Are you hurt?"

Maya was crying into the phone.

"Maya speak to me. Are you alright?"

"Yes. Yes. I'm alright, but something bad has happened. Annika and I wanted to get a soda on our way home, so we walked into this kiosk on the way..." The hitch in Maya's voice made it almost impossible for me to hear what she was saying. My dad entered the kitchen, followed by Helle.

"Is everything alright with Maya?" he asked.

I signaled that they should keep quiet. It was hard to hear what Maya was trying to tell me.

"...this girl...this girl...in the kiosk...she was...Mom, I think she's dead. There's blood all over the place...I..."

"I'll be right there."

26

JULY 1997

The van seemed to drive forever. Nina was so hungry and had such a deep thirst when it finally came to a stop and the door was opened. A man stuck his head in and pulled her out. Nina protested, but he didn't seem to understand any Danish. Either that or he didn't care. Another man helped pull her out and carry her inside a small house on a farm somewhere. There were no other houses in sight.

A door was kicked open and she was thrown on the bare floor. Nina was crying and screaming as the door closed and she heard it lock. Nina got to her feet and hammered her fists against the door while crying for help.

Then she fell to the ground again, wondering why this was happening to her, why these people had the right to treat her like this? She suddenly sensed she wasn't alone in the cold room, and as she raised her head up, she looked into the eyes of several other girls, all children just like herself. Nina wiped her tears away and tried to speak.

"Who are you?"

Three of the girls shook their heads, the rest just kept staring at her. One spoke in a strange language. Nina signaled that she didn't understand. The door opened again and a woman peeked in. She handed Nina a bottle of water and a loaf of bread, then she closed the door again and locked it. Nina drank and ate greedily, while the other girls' eyes rested on her. When she was done, Nina rested her exhausted body by leaning against the wall and trying to sleep.

A few hours later, the door was opened once again. The woman walked in, flanked by two men. They divided the girls into three groups, then told Nina and the two girls in her group to follow her. Nina didn't understand a word of what was being said, but the men pushed her in the right direction and she followed the other girls out of the room. They were led to a room upstairs where five men sat in chairs waiting for them. Frightened, she looked at the woman who spoke a lot of strange words, then pushed Nina ahead, into the middle of the room along with the two other girls. Then she grabbed Nina's blonde hair and showed it to the men and they all smiled and nodded. It felt very uncomfortable for Nina. She was used to people admiring her blonde hair, but not like this. The woman started touching her and taking off her dress. Nina protested and cried, but received a slap across the face as answer. It burned badly and she sobbed, but didn't dare cry out loud anymore. The woman continued to undress her, and soon she was naked in front of the five men, who all seemed very pleased with what they saw. Then the woman spoke a word that Nina understood, since it was very similar to the same word in Danish. She said:

"Dance."

At first, Nina didn't understand. She looked confused at the woman and received another slap across the face. After that, she obeyed. Nina started moving her body and the men all smiled and laughed, one was even clapping his hands. Nina didn't like the way they stared at her body. She felt tears roll down her cheeks, but didn't dare to wipe them away. Her face was still burning from the slaps.

"Dance, dance, dance," the woman repeated again and again. All three girls were now dancing, moving their hips, and the men were clapping and laughing. At that moment, in that room with the fat old men looking at her, Nina learned a valuable lesson. If she was to survive this, she had to perform. So, Nina swung her blonde hair around, causing the men to gasp in awe, and she put her hands on her hips and started moving in circles, receiving applause and many smiles in return. Even the woman clapped as she performed, and afterwards Nina was given a soda and a real meal of chicken and rice for dinner, while the other two girls only got dry bread. She was taken to a room alone where she had a real bed to sleep in, and they even brought her clothes to wear. They didn't look like any clothes Nina had ever worn before. Well, you could hardly call them clothes at all, but at least she knew that she had somehow stood out and made her mark. Nina knew that she was going to be the one who survived this, because she had somehow learned how to play the game.

Nina slept for almost an hour before the door to her room

was opened and the woman entered. She spoke to Nina in words she didn't understand and then let one of the fat old men enter the room. Nina felt her heart beat rapidly as the woman left the room again and left her alone with the man.

"Dance," he said and lifted his arms. "Dance."

So she did. To save her life and get better food than the others and a room to sleep in, she danced, wearing the new clothes they had given her. She danced for the man on the floor next to the bed and saw how she pleased him. After a while, he walked over to her and put his hand on her shoulder to make her stop. Then he ripped off her clothes.

27

———————

APRIL 2013

I took the car, even though I'd had some wine with dinner. I even ran a red light and definitely broke the speed limit on my way downtown towards the kiosk where Maya had called from. She and her friend were still inside when I arrived.

I parked the car outside on the street and ran to the door and knocked on it. Maya had locked it, and as she opened it for me, she burst into tears. Then she threw herself in my arms. Her friend was crying hard too, so I took her in my arms as well.

"She's dead, Mommy..." Maya said in between sobs. "Someone killed her. We came in here to get a soda for the ride home on our bikes and then...we found her like this. We were so scared. We didn't know if he was outside somewhere waiting for us. I was so scared."

"It's okay," I whispered, trying to calm them both down. "Where is she? Where is the body you found?"

"Behind the counter. It's bad, Mom. It's really bad."

"Okay. Lock the door behind me and stay where you are," I said and let go of both of them. "I'll go and look and then we'll call the police, alright? I need to know what to tell them."

Maya sobbed and nodded. "Okay." She and her friend grabbed each other's hands. They were both shaking pretty hard.

I walked closer, bracing myself for what I was about to see, but as I saw it I realized there was no way I could have ever prepared myself for something like this. I covered my mouth with my hand while breathing heavily and fighting the desire to scream. The body was placed behind the counter, in a chair. She was covered in blood and had been stabbed several times in her stomach and chest. All her clothes were soaked, and a pool of blood was on the floor under the chair. I felt sick to my stomach. But worst of all was what he had done to her breast. He had ripped a part of her shirt and her left breast was showing. He had sewed something onto it. I gasped when I realized what it was. A small bowtie. It was white, but the blood had colored it red.

I tried hard to maintain my calm and found my cellphone and called the police. A few minutes later, Officer Morten Bredballe knocked on the door of the kiosk and Maya let him in.

"Where is she?" he asked out of breath as he came up next to me. I pointed and turned my face away. I couldn't hold back my tears any longer and Officer Morten grabbed me just as I was about to collapse.

"Are you alright?" he asked.

"No," I said. "I need to sit down."

I sat down on the floor while the officer took a look at the young girl's bloody body. I heard him gasp and sigh deeply several times as he examined it without touching anything. Then I heard him call for the island's doctor, Doctor Williamsen, to come immediately and bring the ambulance. I managed to get up and walk over to Maya and her friend, and together we walked outside and waited.

Officer Morten joined us a moment later.

"So, who found the body?" he asked.

"My daughter and her friend," I answered.

"Alright. I'll need to take your statement right away. Did you touch anything?"

Maya shook her head. "Just the door."

"Alright. We'll need to get your fingerprints to be able to distinguish between yours and the killer's. Then I'll need to get your statements. But first we must wait for Doctor Williamsen to declare her death and I have to call for the forensic department from the mainland to come and examine the place. I'll probably need to call in more officers tomorrow. As if we didn't have enough on our hands right now."

"The girl," I said. "Did you ever find her?"

Officer Morten shook his head. "No. I'm afraid we didn't. She seems to have vanished into thin air. I just don't get it, you know? This is an island, for Christ sake. There aren't that many places she could be."

"Could the kidnappers have taken her to the mainland?"

Officer Morten nodded. "That is a possibility. I mean, we are checking all cars that leave the island by ferry, and the staff working at the ferry is keeping an eye out for anything, but to be honest, they could have had a boat ready and sailed right towards the mainland without us ever knowing it."

"And now this, huh? Is there a surveillance tape that might help see who did this?" I asked hopefully. I really didn't like to think that this guy was out there somewhere waiting for his next victim. This was nasty and the girl wasn't much older than Maya. It scared the dickens out of me.

"That was the first thing I checked for," Officer Morten said. "Unfortunately, it's gone. Whoever did this took it with him."

"Whoever did this has done something like it before," I mumbled, as Officer Morten received a call on his cellphone.

28

APRIL 2013

I drove Maya to the police station the next morning to have her fingerprints taken. She was tired and still quite shocked when we got into the car. After taking her statement, Officer Morten had let us go home and get some sleep. I had driven Maya's friend Annika home and explained everything to her parents before finally being able to bring my own daughter home and let my dad get back to his house.

Maya had wanted to sleep in my room, so we shared my bed for the night, and neither of us got much sleeping done. Instead, we ended up talking most of the night. It had been years since I had felt this close to my daughter, and even though the circumstances were extremely horrible and sad, I was happy to have been there, to be the one to take care of her. We had truly bonded that night, even about her dad and how she sometimes cried when I didn't see it because she missed him and hated the fact that he never wanted to see her because of his new wife. I cursed Michael far away while comforting my daughter.

"How are you doing?" I asked, after starting the engine. "Are you okay with all of this?"

"I just want to get it over with so I can return to my normal life," she said, nodding. I spotted something on her arm.

"What's that?"

She looked down, then shook her head. "It's nothing. It's Patrick's autograph."

"You met him?"

"Just briefly, close to the hotel. He gave us both an autograph. He was really nice," she said.

"Well, good for you," I said, and put the car in gear. "At least you got something out of last night."

I parked outside of the police station and grabbed my daughter's hand as we walked towards the entrance of the small police station. I smiled, thinking about when we had first come to the island and picked up the key to our new house here. It was no more than eight months ago, yet it felt like a lifetime. I could hardly remember what my life was like before Fanoe Island. I thought about my book and was so grateful that it had sold so well all over the country. That gave me the freedom to be with my family and take care of them the way I had always wanted to. It was great that I didn't have some boss to answer to on a day like this when my daughter needed me.

"I still keep seeing her sitting there on that chair," she suddenly said as I grabbed the door handle and was about to open the door for her. "It was like she could still see me, you know? I know it sounds weird, but I kept expecting her to move or to try and say something. I keep wondering, what if she wasn't dead when we walked in? What if she was still breathing and wanted to tell us who had done this to her, but she couldn't move her lips? How horrifying would that be?"

I reached over and stroked her hair. "I know you'll be thinking a lot about this for some time to come, but try not to let your imagination run off with you, sweetie."

"Yeah, but that's the problem, Mom. It's really difficult. I mean, she was about my age, right? A little older, but still. And the guy is still out there, here on the island. Will he do it again? Will it be someone I know the next time?"

"Sweetie. You need to relax. We have no idea what went on before this. Maybe he knew her. Maybe he was an old boyfriend that she had recently broken up with; maybe he was jealous. You never know. But you can't let fear ruin your life and keep you from doing things you like and living your life."

Maya sighed and let me hold the door for her as she entered, while mumbling, "You're right, Mom."

Inside, Officer Morten was very sweet to Maya and took her through all the procedures while telling her with a kind voice what he was doing and why. When they came back to me, she was smiling for the first time since last night.

"What's so funny?" I asked.

"Oh, we were just talking about the TV show and the auditions tomorrow. Officer Morten has a daughter who is going. She's sixteen, so it's her last chance to audition. He thinks she'll win the whole thing and make him rich so he doesn't have to hunt criminals anymore. I told him that if a sixteen-year-old gets rich she's probably not going to share it all with him. She might give him a new car or something, but that's probably it."

I chuckled and gave Maya her jacket. She was so pale from lack of sleep and the shock. It worried me to see her like this. "Do you have any leads, Officer?" I asked.

He looked exhausted, as well, and I was guessing that he hadn't slept, either. "No, not so far. No one saw anyone enter the kiosk last night around the time we suspect the killer entered, and no one saw him leave either. But the bowtie sewed onto her breast has been seen before. The police on the mainland have been looking for a killer for several years who sews a bowtie onto his victims just like that. They call him the bowtie killer. It's very original, I know."

"The bowtie killer?" I exclaimed. "I remember hearing about him. Yes, that's right. Last year I think it was, he killed a girl in Roskilde, I think it was, and that was when they started writing about him in the press. I had completely forgotten about that. I guess since we haven't heard anything for a long time, that I thought he was gone somehow. So, he's still on the loose? Do you think he's still on the island?"

"It's not very likely," Officer Morten said. "A killer as clever as he is wouldn't stay in the same place for long. My colleagues who are working on this case have told me that he has never struck in the same place twice so far. He's long gone if you ask me. Probably took the last ferry out last night, or maybe even had his own boat ready."

I nodded, thinking I should feel more relieved, but I still couldn't shake this unease inside of me.

What if he's still out there? Lurking, waiting to find his next victim, his next prey.

"And what about the little girl?" I asked.

"No news yet."

"Could she have run away? I mean the life of a Countess can be pretty strict and not much fun for a child, right?"

"I probably shouldn't tell you all this, but since you know so much already, I guess it's no harm. The thing is, she did run away. She ran from her teacher and nanny, down to the beach, probably because she just wanted a little fun. Then this dogwalker came along, and for some reason she walked away with him."

"Did anyone see the dog? What kind it was?" my clever daughter asked.

"It was a German shepherd, but don't run around and start questioning everyone with a German shepherd, promise me that?"

My daughter laughed and nodded. It was good to see her happy again. I was so afraid that last night's event would push her into some sort of post traumatic stress disorder or something. I had been wondering if I should take her to see a therapist to talk about all the things she had been through lately, but now at this moment at the police station she seemed to be doing okay. I could still sense the sadness that the shock had left her with, but something inside of me, call it a mother's intuition or whatever, told me she was going to be alright. She could handle this.

"Say, I know a woman who lost her daughter some years ago, you know the woman Helle who has a store downtown?"

"I know Helle, yes. Most unfortunate what happened to her

daughter. It was in 2005, as far as I recall. But she drowned. That was the conclusion of the investigation, if I remember correctly. I wasn't here back then. I was stationed in Northern Jutland before I was transferred to Fanoe Island three years ago."

"But they don't know, do they? They never found the body?" I asked.

Officer Morten sighed. "I think I know where you're going with this, and I might as well stop you right there. On this island, children disappear from time to time. They walk into the water and are sucked out. This has always happened and it happens because parents do not look out for their children properly. If they go out there in the ocean alone, thinking they can make it to the island and the tides come in, they drown. Doesn't matter how good a swimmer you are, even an adult can be sucked out."

"But what happens to their bodies? Why aren't they found?"

He shrugged with a tired look. "Who knows? They get pulled out far enough they never return. That's just the way it is. All I can say is, watch those kids of yours; don't let them wander off."

"Lets' go, Mom. I'm tired," Maya said and pulled my sleeve.

"Okay, Maya," Officer Morten said. "You're done here and I'll be in touch if we have further questions."

"Thank you, Officer," I said and turned to walk out. As I reached the front door and was about to open it, I suddenly stopped and turned to face Officer Morten again.

"One last question, Officer. Have any of the children disappearing from this island been boys or has it only been girls?"

29

APRIL 2013

Naturally, Officer Morten couldn't answer my question, so I took it home to my computer. Maya went to her room to get some sleep while I started researching the missing children of Fanoe Island. That was when a title popped into my head.

"Lost: The Story of the Missing Children of Fanoe Island," I said out loud and smiled. It needed a little work, but as a working title, it was great. Something told me there was a story here to be told. Maybe if I interviewed the families whose children had gone missing, I could start to piece it together? It was definitely a start.

I searched the Internet for missing children and Fanoe, and soon found two articles dated back to 2005—one in the local paper and one in a paper from the mainland—about the loss of Helle's daughter.

Vadehavet demands another child and *Fanoe loses yet*

another child to the sea. According to the articles, it had been several years since the ocean last took a child, not since the late nineties, it stated. The coast guard was quoted saying that it was very important for parents to watch their children constantly to avoid these kinds of accidents from happening. *Only a fool doesn't fear the ocean,* the coast guard officer was quoted saying.

Then there was a discussion whether or not the Danish beaches should have lifeguards, something they still hadn't established, for some reason, and something they still discussed from time to time, but never agreed upon. It always came down to the money. Who was going to pay for it? The cities? The counties? The government? Denmark was nothing but beaches all over, and it would be an expensive affair to provide all of them with lifeguards. No one wanted to take the responsibility upon themselves. I had never understood that. They could tell us not to smoke and how to eat right by putting extra taxes on cigarettes and fat in the food, and even forbid people to smoke anywhere, but put up a few lifeguards to prevent people from drowning (which someone did every year, especially German tourists who didn't know the ocean) they wouldn't do.

I sighed and leaned back in my chair, wondering if there could be any connection between the disappearance of the little Countess and the brutal killing of a teenager in a kiosk last night. I chuckled and shook my head. How on earth should that even be possible? No, the bowtie killer was long gone; Officer Morten was probably right about that. But the girl was still missing, and there was something not adding up about all these children supposedly drowning.

The phone rang and I picked it up. It was Officer Morten.

"I kept thinking about what you asked me this morning," he said. "I have enough to do today as it is, but it kept haunting me, so I looked into it."

I sat up straight in my chair, sensing something interesting was coming. "Yes. And what did you find?"

"Well, you were right. We don't have records further back, but in 1997-1998 four children went missing and were later declared dead by drowning. And then there was the one in 2005. All of them were girls. And, get this. All of them were six years old when they went missing. And all of them had long blonde hair and blue eyes. I have the pictures here from their files and they look very much alike."

I almost dropped my jaw. "That can't be a coincidence," I said.

"Something tells me you're right."

"I mean a lot of Danish children have blonde hair and blue eyes, but to have all five kids look like that? And then have the same age and gender? It's a little too obvious, if you ask me." I wrote everything down while talking to the Officer. I had butterflies in my stomach. We were definitely on to something here. Something big.

"Someone has been stealing our children," he said. "And probably killing them, too. The worst part is, they've gotten away with it so far, since no one saw the connection."

"The question is, does that someone also have Josephine?" I asked.

Officer Morten exhaled into the phone. "That's what we need to find out now. And we need to do it fast."

30

APRIL 2013

"You made the front cover again," Hanne said, and threw a newspaper on the table next to the croissants that Patrick was eating. They were in his room and he was wearing nothing but a bathrobe and sunglasses.

Patrick looked above his sunglasses and scanned the front page with a grin. It showed a huge picture of him standing outside on the balcony the night before, balancing the railing on the three-story building with his arms stretched in the air, not holding on to anything.

"Well, the producers are very pleased that you're creating all this publicity. But please don't be foolish, alright? Attention is good, but not if it means we lose you."

Patrick gulped down his coffee and stopped listening to what she said. Instead, another article on the front page had caught his interest. It was just a small one and there was no picture, but the headline drew him in.

Kiosk Girl Killed by Bowtie Killer.

Patrick smiled widely and read the article discreetly, while Hanne was still babbling on about ratings and shares and the importance of the coming days. He felt a spark of thrill in his body as he read about the girl who had allegedly been stabbed to death and had a bowtie sewn onto one breast, the signature mark of the bowtie killer. The police were quoted saying that if anyone had seen anything around the time of the girl's death, they would be most grateful to know, even the smallest thing might be of importance, the officer said. Patrick laughed out loud and leaned back in his chair, thinking he had once again done it without leaving a trace behind.

They're never gonna catch me. I'm always ahead of them. Stupid morons. I'm just too freaking smart.

Hanne stopped talking and looked at him.

"Are you even listening to what I'm saying?" she said curtly.

Patrick looked at her behind his sunglasses and could hardly see her in the darkness. Then he grinned, while imagining snapping her throat again. It always put him in a better mood, thinking how easily he could kill her, how little an effort it would take on his part.

Women are so feeble, so weak, and faint. Useless, really. Can't even put up a fight. So easy to hurt. How I loathe them. All of them. With their pretty faces and swaying hips, always trying to make me like them, to flirt with me. As if I cared. If only they knew what really turned me on.

Hanne snapped her fingers in front of Patrick's face. "Hello? Are you there?" she asked.

Patrick growled. Her attitude towards him was starting to get really annoying. Didn't she know that without him she had no job? She was nothing without him; this show was nothing.

Patrick grinned and looked up at her. "Sure," he said. "I'm always here, aren't I? It's not like there would be anywhere else I could go."

"Good," Hanne said. "It's an important day tomorrow and we need to get things up and running smoothly. Today, you rest, alright?"

"You got it," he said, and took a huge bite of his croissant. He leaned back and put his feet up on the table.

"Good," Hanne said and took her notepad. "Oh, yes, and the police want to see you, they're waiting outside. I told them to keep it brief since you need your rest."

Patrick almost choked on his croissant. Hanne opened the door and two police officers entered the room. Patrick got up from his chair.

"This is Officer Gammelgaard and Officer Nyberg. They're with the National homicide team in Copenhagen," Hanne said.

They shook hands. Patrick was still fighting the food stuck in his throat. He couldn't stop coughing.

"Are you alright there?" the younger one of the two, Officer Gammelgaard asked.

"I'll be fine," Patrick said, still coughing. "Just got a little something down the wrong pipe."

Hanne patted him on the back and soon Patrick was able to stop coughing. "Sit down, gentlemen," he said, and showed them to the couches in his suite. He glanced one last time at the story of the girl on the newspaper cover before he turned to face them. Patrick put on his famous smile and looked at them.

"So what can I do for you gentlemen?"

31

APRIL 2013

The floor of the dog cage was hard, and after almost two days in it, Josephine's body had started to hurt badly. She tried to move around, but it was so small that there weren't many positions she could use, and stretching her legs was out of the question. The bucket she used as a toilet was beginning to smell and it left her with constant nausea. She hadn't seen the old lady all morning and hoped that she would bring her food today, since Josephine was really hungry now. All she had gotten up until now was the water in the bowl that she had to drink like a dog. At some point, the lady had to bring her some food, didn't she?

Josephine whimpered, feeling awful, her stomach hurting from starvation, her breathing complicated by the strong odor emanating from the bucket. She grabbed the door to the cage once again and tried to shake it, but she knew it was useless. She wasn't strong enough to break the lock or even bend the door.

She had tried everything, even hammering her fists into it as hard as she could, and she didn't even make a dent in the bars. They barely even rattled at all.

Finally, the door opened and the woman walked in with her dog behind her. She was humming that awful nursery rhyme about a woman and her sick dolly that Ms. Camilla had sometimes sung for Josephine when she was younger. The woman closed the door and locked it as soon as the dog was inside. Django walked over to Josephine and sniffed her through the bars.

"Phew, you're right, Django," the old lady said and held her nose. "It does stink in here."

With a stick in her hand, the lady unlocked the cage and opened the door. With her heart in her throat, Josephine thought this was it, this was her moment to escape. But as soon as she tried to move, the lady poked her with the stick in the stomach hard, and it forced her to fall backwards.

"Django," the woman yelled. "Make sure it stays in there."

Django became alert. He walked closer to the opening, then growled at Josephine, snapping his teeth at her. Josephine was gasping for air while the lady leaned in, grabbed the bucket, and removed it. Barely had Josephine caught her breath from the blow before the old woman was out again and had closed the door. Django was still standing outside the cage, staring at her, like he was making sure she didn't move. Josephine cried and whimpered.

"Please give me something to eat. I'm so hungry. Please," she begged, while the woman disappeared with the bucket in her hand. Django was still watching her. The woman returned a little while later with the bucket in one hand and a hose in the other.

"Let's get rid of that awful stench; shall we, Django, huh?"

Then she hosed Josephine down with a river of water that made Josephine believe she was going to drown. She gasped for air and swallowed loads of water. She was still coughing when the hose was turned off. Then the lady opened the cage again and threw in the bucket.

"There. That should keep you clean for a little while," she said, and locked the door again. Josephine watched as the lady rolled the hose back, then left and returned with a towel and something else in her hand. She knelt in front of Josephine and seemed to be examining her. She reached in and grabbed her arm and pulled it out through the bars to better look at it. Josephine gasped and started to cry again. "Please, don't hurt me," she said.

The woman didn't answer. She studied her skin closely and turned her arm in the light. "Yes, Django. I do believe you're right. The baby doll's skin has become looser." The lady now threw in the towel and the other thing she had in her hand.

"Dry yourself off and then apply this lotion to your skin," she said to Josephine.

She grabbed her chin and looked her in the eyes. Then she smiled. "So soft the skin is on my darling baby doll," she said, and stroked her cheek. "Yes, we need the skin to stay that way, to stay soft and smooth, don't we, Django? Yes, we do."

The woman got up and walked away, then returned with the box of fake eyes. While Josephine applied the lotion to her skin, the woman found a pair of eyes and held them up. Then she signaled Josephine to come closer to the bars. Thinking that maybe if she was nice to the woman she would give her something to eat, Josephine obeyed. She put her head against the bars and let the lady study her eyes closely, while holding a pair of fake eyes up next to her face.

Then she shook her head. "No, you're right, Django. Not quite the right color. Let's see if I have another one that will fit better. How about this one?" she said and found a new pair that she held up.

"Yes, those are the ones," she said with a shrill voice. "They will be perfect for my new baby doll."

32

APRIL 2013

Maya was still sleeping when there was a knock at the front door. I ran downstairs to see who it was. It was Jack and he was smiling.

"Ready?" he asked.

"The shop! I completely forgot," I said. "We were going to visit Helle's shop today."

Jack looked disappointed.

"Just give me one minute and I'll be there," I said and rushed inside. I threw on a new blouse and decided that jeans would be fine. It was a little windy outside and very cloudy, so I took my jacket and an umbrella as well, just in case. I wrote a note for Maya and put it on the kitchen table, then hurried outside to meet Jack.

He smiled when he saw me. "Do you want to walk down there?"

"Sure," I said and closed my jacket when the cold wind hit my chest.

It took fifteen minutes to walk into town. It was nice to get out of the house and get some fresh air for a change. Plus, I enjoyed Jack's company. He was the outdoorsy type; you could tell just by looking at him. He liked it when the tip of his nose turned red and the wind bit his cheeks. And he was funny, too. Made me laugh out loud several times on our way there. He always made me feel so comfortable in his presence. It was a quality I had grown to like in a man more than anything. Especially since my failed marriage to Michael, Victor and Maya's father. Ever since he left me, I had come to realize that he wasn't good for me. Being with him had somehow dragged me down, made me insecure about myself. Michael was a fault finder, especially with people, and in particular with me. He never thought I looked good, or at least he never told me. Instead, he would always pick some other woman at the party or in the restaurant and ask me why I didn't wear my hair like that or why I didn't exercise more to look like her. It wasn't all the time, but just small hints here and there, enough to make me constantly feel lousy about myself when I was with him. While married to him, I thought that it was okay, that it was just the way it was, that if I just changed, then he would be happy again, but after he left me I realized that it wouldn't have mattered what I had done or not done. It would have never been enough for him.

"A penny for your thoughts?" Jack said.

"Sorry?"

"You went quiet all of a sudden. I was just wondering what was on your mind."

"Ah. Well, lots of things, to be honest with you. Just now I was actually thinking about my ex-husband."

Jack nodded. "Ah, I see. Dddo you miss him?"

I shrugged. "Not really, I guess. I miss him being a father for my children. I miss having a father figure in their lives, but me? I think I'm better off without him. Besides, he is married to someone else now."

"But if he wasn't, would you miss him?" Jack asked.

I looked at his handsome face. He had the gentlest eyes I had ever seen. "I don't know," I said. "I think he has disappointed me so much that it is hard to still care. But I do miss being a family. I think I will always miss that."

Jack went quiet.

"What about you?" I asked.

"What about me?"

"Do you have someone you miss in your life?"

"Nah. I've given up my life to take care of my sister."

I felt a pinch in my heart. That was so sad. "But don't you want a family? A wife? Children?"

Jack nodded slowly and thoughtfully. "Sure. I've always wanted that. And I've had my share of female friendships."

"But never anything serious?" I asked.

He looked at me. "There was one. We went out for almost a year." Jack sighed and looked away. I thought about grabbing his hand, but restrained myself. We walked up the cobbled street in the middle of the town. Small shops lined the road up ahead. One of them was Helle's.

"What happened?" I asked.

"Well, she wanted to move on with the relationship. She wanted to move in together. I told her she could come live at our house, and so she did. But she soon grew tired of it. She wanted me to put my sister in a home. She was waking her up at night with her moaning and crying in pain. She was annoyed with me for constantly taking care of my sister instead of her. Stuff like that. Finally, she told me it was her or my sister. I told her I had made a promise to myself to take care of my sister, and I wasn't going to break that promise."

"So she left?"

"So she left, yes. Ever since then, I've been very careful and I never bring anyone to my house anymore. It's always the same. They want me to put my sister in a home so we can build a life together. I tell them I can't and then they're gone. So, eventually, I've kind of just accepted the fact that maybe I won't get that big family with all the children I dreamt of. Well, I can always borrow one of Sophia's, right? I mean, she has plenty."

I laughed, but not joyfully. Jack's story made me so sad.

"I think it's here," he said and looked up at a sign above a small shop.

It said *Dolls and Trinkets*.

33

APRIL 2013

"**H**I GUYS!"

Helle smiled and came out from the back as we entered the store. It was a small, dark room swamped with trinkets and souvenirs on all the shelves and in aisles in the middle.

"Wow," I said, as I looked around the inviting shop.

"Yes," Helle said with a smile. "Welcome to my small shop. This is my pride and joy."

My eyes fell on the back row and the maybe fifty dolls sitting on the shelves staring at me. I felt a chill on my spine. Dolls as lifelike as these had always creeped me out.

"Come and look at them closer," Helle said, and walked towards them. She picked one and pulled it down. It was the size of a child of maybe six years and looked completely like it was alive. The eyes especially looked so real.

"Wow," I said again and studied it closer. "I can't believe how real it looks. There's even a little sparkle in her eyes. And the hair..." I reached over and touched it, but Helle pulled it away. "Sorry," she said and pointed at a sign behind her that said *Please don't touch the dolls.* "No touching, please. I don't want them to be greasy and dirty from people's fingers."

"Oh, okay. Well, they're really...lifelike."

Helle hugged the one she was holding then looked at its face. "They're my babies." She put her finger on the doll's nose and pretended to be talking to a child. "Yes you are, cutie pie, yes you're my baby doll."

I cleared my throat. Helle stopped herself and put the doll back. I forced a smile.

"So, wwwhat do you want me to pppaint?" Jack asked, stuttering slightly again. He was nervous.

Helle smiled widely. "I want you to do five paintings of five dolls. I want you to make them as a portrait of a living person. I'll pick the dolls and give them to you. I'll pay you well. Five thousand for each painting."

Jack gasped. His eyes grew wide. "Five thousand? That's too much..."

"No, no," Helle interrupted him. "I know you're the best for the job. I don't mind paying a little extra to get something extraordinary. You're definitely worth it."

Jack blushed. "Wwwell tthank you, then."

"You're welcome. Here is the first doll I want you to create a portrait of," she said, and pulled down one with blonde hair and blue eyes. "I just need to make her look real pretty." Helle put a new light blue dress on the doll. Then she found a brush and started fixing her hair, then pulled out a light blue bowtie and put it on the side of the hair. My heart stopped when I saw the bowtie. Could it be? I walked closer and looked at it. It seemed to be exactly like the one I had seen the night before, the one that had been sewn onto that poor girl's breast. I was shocked at first, but then figured that you could probably buy the exact same bowties in many doll stores around the country and that the police had probably already looked into that. But why did the bowtie killer do that to his victims? Was it to tell us something?

I watched as Helle finished the doll up and we followed her into the back. She had arranged a small scene with a landscape in the background and a chair in the middle. Helle now placed the doll in the chair and walked backwards.

"There is the painting I want," she said. "With her like that and then the landscape in the background. Make her look as alive as you can." Helle paused, then spoke again. "Isn't she adorable? She looks just like my girl did on the day when she..."

Helle stopped and I could tell she was fighting back tears. "She would have been fourteen next month if she..." Helle picked up a photo of her daughter in a lovely frame from a shelf and showed it to me. My heart dropped and I put my hand on Helle's shoulder. Her baby girl would have been Maya's age by now. I couldn't bear to think about it. I didn't even want to imagine what it had to feel like. To think of losing Maya when she was only six? Oh, my God, it was unbearable. The horror of losing your child by far surpassed anything I could ever imagine.

"I was thinking you would come here and paint her," Helle said and sniffled. "I prefer that she doesn't leave the store."

"Okay," Jack said and nodded. "I'll start first thing tomorrow."

As we left Helle's shop, I felt horrible inside. I felt bad for

Helle and what had happened to her and I couldn't stop thinking about what Officer Morten had told me about the disappearances maybe not being drowning accidents after all. I could hardly tell Helle, since it was just speculation so far, but part of me wanted to give her some hope that maybe her daughter was out there somewhere, that maybe, just maybe there was a slight possibility that she could still be alive.

34

JULY 2001

It was her birthday, but no one at the brothel knew or even cared. Nina turned ten years old doing what she had done dozens of times a day the last four years: being raped by old fat guys who especially asked for her because of her blonde hair and fair skin. She was a specialty; she'd realized that by now. A pearl in the sea. The people keeping her locked up were making a fortune on her. She was the star of the place, the one attracting the most men.

Yet, no one even cared to celebrate her on her big day. As usual, Nina worked all night and didn't go to sleep before five in the morning. She danced for the men and let them touch her, assault her, even hurt her, just because she knew that as long as she gave them what they wanted, she'd stay alive. The more men she pleased, the more and better she ate and lived. On days when the customers weren't pleased, she didn't eat at all. Just one complaint and they would take her food, and sometimes even slap her around in her room till she understood how to behave.

They had given her a new name. Miss Cha-Cha, they called her. Because of her dancing skills that allured so many men. Nina had, little by little, learned to understand the language. She hadn't forgotten her native Danish, since she had practiced it every time she had a few minutes between clients, while laying alone in her bed, enjoying the rare moment of peace, crying, remembering her mother and trying hard to forgive her for giving her away. But it was becoming harder and harder as she grew older, and soon a hatred for her mother grew inside of her, poisoning her mind.

And so it was this morning on her tenth birthday that Nina lay down on her bed, her legs sore from dancing all night, her insides sore from being misused again and again. Her cheeks sore from the slapping of her face that many men enjoyed when they *played* with her, as they called it. So it was that Nina looked back at her life before she was sent away and remembered all the details of her mother's face, even the house on the street that she had grown up in, and decided that some day, one day in the near future, she was going to go back. Somehow, she was going to escape this hellhole.

Nina cried thinking about her hometown and the life she'd had before her mother decided to send her away. She even remembered the name of the island that she grew up on. *Fanoe Island.* And even though she knew it was far away from Poland, she knew she was going back there one day, if it was the last thing she ever did.

Nina jumped out of bed and walked down the hall and

into the shower that was shared by all twelve girls on the floor. She turned it on extremely hot, then walked in. It was so warm it was painful, but that was how she wanted it to be. After a long night of working, she always took burning hot showers. She had this idea that it somehow cleansed her of all the smells, of the germs put there by the smelly, stinky old men. And she wanted to be clean. More than anything, Nina wanted to be cleansed of the atrocities committed against her. She felt so dirty, so besmirched, and no matter how much she washed herself and scrubbed her body with soap, the feeling wouldn't go away.

Nina found the bath brush and started to scrub her skin. She rubbed and rubbed, and soon her legs started bleeding. But that didn't stop her. She continued scrubbing, while crying and sobbing, in the burning hot shower.

"I hate you. I hate you," she yelled, thinking of her mother's face, hearing her mother's words inside of her head. She looked down at her stomach and legs and felt like screaming, but restrained herself, since she didn't want to alert the guards by the doors downstairs. They would just come in here and have their way with her as well. She had learned that lesson when she had gotten into a fight with another girl in the bathroom and they had come running. They had locked the door and then raped both of the girls for hours, taking turns until the girls could hardly walk. Then they had sent them to their room for ten minutes before a customer was sent up there.

Nina had come to hate her body, to loathe everything about it. All the things that made her successful in the brothel, she hated. Even her long blonde hair that they all adored so much.

But, most of all, she hated the fact that she was beginning to look like her mother.

Nina walked out of the shower and glanced at herself in the reflection of the window. She could see it a little more every day. Even though her mother wasn't blonde and fair like her, she could still see her when she looked at herself. See her in her features...her nose, her chin, and even sometimes in her eyes. It made her furious.

"One day, Mommy dear, I'll be back," she told her own reflection. "And then I'll kill you," she mumbled. "That's my promise to you. I'll make you suffer like you have caused me to suffer, and then I'll kill you."

35

APRIL 2013

"Now, I don't know if you've heard about what happened last night here on the island?" Officer Nyberg said.

Patrick leaned over, feeling a sudden thrill inside of him. Had they finally caught up with him? Had they really figured it out? "I don't think I know what you're talking about."

The second officer took over. "Officer Nyberg and I are working on the bowtie killer case. Maybe you've heard about him?"

Patrick felt like laughing out loud, but held it back. This was ridiculous. Were they really here talking to him about this with absolutely no clue at all? Were they really that stupid? Apparently.

"No, I don't believe I have," Patrick said with a smirk.

Officer Gammelgaard cleared his throat. "Well, in the last couple of years, we have been trying to track down this killer who...well, kills people, girls, around the country by stabbing them and then..." Officer Gammelgaard seemed to feel sick all of a sudden. It amused Patrick immensely.

Officer Nyberg took over. "He sews these small bowties onto his victims' breasts afterwards and then leaves them."

"Oh, wow. That sounds horrible," Patrick said, and took off his sunglasses to show how sympathetic he really was. He looked into their eyes. "Do you have any idea who he is, any idea at all?"

The two officers looked at one another. Officer Gammelgaard answered while the other one sighed. "Uh, to be frank, we don't have much yet."

"And this has been going on for how many years?" Patrick asked.

"Two. At least, that we know of. There might be more that we just haven't found yet."

"Alright. But what does that have to do with me, gentlemen?" Patrick asked, leaning back in his chair and looking at his watch.

"Well, there is one connection that we're looking into," Officer Nyberg continued.

"And what might that be?"

"It seems the killer chooses towns that your TV show has just been to or is at when he kills. Like last night." Officer Nyberg cleared his throat again.

"So, what are you saying? Do you think it's someone from the show?" Patrick asked, feigning incredulity.

"No, not that. It's just that we think the killer might be somehow connected or maybe even obsessed with the TV show. Or maybe he wants to cover up the killings by choosing the towns where your show is or has just been because no one will notice anyone with strange behavior when the town is full of people coming from all over to see the show. It's easy to hide in a crowd."

"Plus, he seems to have a preference for younger women, several of them have been teenagers, and wherever your show is, there are many teenagers," Officer Gammelgaard said.

"Hmm," Patrick said, holding a hand to his chin, trying to look pensive, like he was taking this very seriously. He was quite impressed with his own acting.

"It might also be some sort of stalker of your show," Officer Nyberg continued. "Or maybe even of you."

"I see," Patrick said. "Have you discussed this matter with the producers?"

"Yes," Hanne interrupted. She had been sitting by the dining table, eating the rest of Patrick's breakfast and reading the paper while they talked. Patrick had almost forgotten she was still there. He turned his head and looked at her. She was putting jelly on her croissant and some of it dripped down on the plate. Patrick thought it looked like the blood dripping on the floor and remembered how the girl's blood had dripped the night before in the kiosk.

"And what did they say?" he asked.

Hanne shrugged. "We can't do much about it, can we? There are lunatics all over the country. We can't stop the TV show just because of this."

Patrick turned and looked at the officers. "You heard the lady. The show must go on," He replied, flashing the officers his best smile.

"Yes, well we're aware of that, but for now we're just telling you this to make you aware of what is going on. We will be present at the auditions tomorrow, looking for anything suspicious, and for the rest of the time you and your crew are here on the island we will be here, too. Just to make sure the killer doesn't strike again."

Patrick smiled and put on his sunglasses again. "No, we couldn't have that, now could we?"

36

APRIL 2013

Sophia came over early on Saturday morning. I was preparing breakfast when the first of her kids stormed through the door. Three-year-old Jonathan had snot running from his nose and crackers in his hands when he came into the kitchen with a huge grin.

"Hi there, little buddy," I said.

He gave my leg a warm hug like only he knew how to. It made me laugh. I stroked his hair and he looked up at me with rosy red cheeks and glassy eyes.

"Maya?" he said.

"Maya will be down in a few seconds. Until then, sit down and have a freshly baked breakfast roll."

Jonathan smiled and proceeded to climb up on a chair to grab one from the table. He started eating it, throwing crumbs all over the floor to add to the cracker bits already deposited there upon his arrival. I decided not to care.

"Maya?" he said again with his mouth full.

"Just give her a minute, sweetie."

The front door opened and Sophia's face appeared. She had the baby in a sling around her chest and the rest of her kids following tailing her. She spotted Jonathan with the roll in his hand and heaved a sigh of relief. "There you are. I couldn't find you, Jonathan. You can't leave the house all by yourself." She looked up at me. "I'm so sorry for that."

"It's okay," I said. "You know I enjoy having him here."

"He has just been so looking forward to spending time with Maya again. She's all he talks about lately."

I chuckled and put butter and cheese on the table. "I know how much he loves her. She is very fond of him too, so I'm sure they're going to have a great day together." I spotted Christoffer and Ida in their nice clothes and water-combed hair. I offered them a roll each. Christoffer took one, Ida shook her head.

"She's too nervous to eat," Sophia said. "I tried all morning."

"Well, maybe I'll bring some of these babies in a bag for later, then?" I said and winked at Ida.

She smiled and nodded a little shyly. Jonathan grabbed my scarf from the chair and started pulling it. The chair tipped over and hit his sister, Anne, on the toes. Anne started crying and yelled at Jonathan. Sophia grabbed Jonathan and Anne and dragged them into the living room. Maya showed up on the stairs. Something broke in the living room as it hit the floor.

I sighed while picking up the chair and the scarf from the floor. I looked into my daughter's eyes. She seemed unusually awake for this hour of the day on a Saturday. I grabbed her face between my hands and kissed her forehead. I looked into her eyes. "Are you sure you're up for this? It's gonna be hard."

"I'm fine, Mom. I know these kids, remember?"

"I called Grandpa and asked him to come over too, to help you out a little. He might be bringing Helle. They'll be here as soon as possible."

"Great. Where is Victor?"

"He's in the yard already. I think he might be planning on spending all day out there. You know, staying away from the noise and trouble. He's not happy with me leaving him with a house filled with kids, but as long as he's able to play on his own, I don't think he'll even notice I'm gone. We'll be back in a couple of hours."

Maya shrugged and grabbed a roll. A scream emerged from the living room as Jonathan came running towards Maya in the kitchen. He threw himself at her leg and hugged it tight. I couldn't stop smiling. Maya picked him up, propped him on her hip, and started kissing his cheeks. Jonathan whined with joy. Maya laughed, too. I enjoyed watching the two of them together while finishing my coffee and packing up some breakfast rolls for later. I left a bunch for Maya to feed to the kids while we were gone. Maya grabbed a second one and ate it standing with Jonathan. He put his head on her shoulder and looked at her with deep affection in his eyes.

Sophia looked exhausted as she walked back into the kitchen. The baby was fussing in the sling. She hushed her baby girl Alma and rocked her entire body trying to get the baby to fall asleep.

"Do you want anything to eat?" I asked her. "I bet you had no time to get anything yourself this morning?"

Sophia smiled. "Yes, please. That would be nice."

I buttered a roll and poured her a cup of coffee, and she ate while I finished getting ready. My dad and Helle showed up right as we were about to leave.

"Perfect timing," I said and kissed my dad. I gave Helle a hug. "Victor is in the yard playing and the rest of the kids are... well, everywhere else. We'll hopefully be back in a couple of hours."

"Don't worry about it," he said. "We'll have fun."

"Yeah, I love kids," Helle said and smiled. It had a great sadness to it and I felt bad once again. I couldn't stop thinking about her daughter and all the other girls that had disappeared on this island. Was it even a good idea to start digging into this, or was I only going to inflict even more pain on those who were involved?

I wasn't sure.

37

———————

APRIL 2013

We arrived at the auditions early, but it was still really hard to find a parking place. The place was jam-packed with people, mostly young teenagers and children with their parents. It was taking place in the old theater downtown and the line outside went around the building into the street and blocked all traffic. I was stunned, to put it mildly. I didn't even know that there were that many people on the entire island.

"Lots of people came in with the ferry last night and this morning from the mainland to participate, as well," Sophia said, as we found a spot in the back of the line.

I sighed, thinking this was going to take a lot more than just a couple of hours. Maybe this wasn't such a great idea after all.

"I'm so glad you're here with us," Sophia said.

Ida nodded and grabbed my hand. I put my arm around her and hugged her. She was the quietest one of Sophia's kids. I was wondering if she even wanted to do this audition. She was usually so shy. Sophia had told me that Ida had wanted to come, that she was the one who had asked first if she could audition, and then Christoffer had said that he wanted to do it, too. I found it hard to believe. It was so unlike her. I felt bad that she didn't even have anything to eat. I pulled out a bag of gummy worms and opened it. I asked her if she wanted one and she refused even those.

Poor thing, I thought, and put one in my mouth. I loved the taste of gummy worms. I offered Christoffer one and he took three. I put one in Sophia's mouth while she was still rocking the baby back and forth.

"Thanks," she said with her mouth full. "Hit the sweet spot."

I chuckled. The line in front of us was hardly moving. I ate another handful of gummy worms. Good thing it was one of the big bags with this line. I put the bag back with the rest of the food arsenal I had brought.

"Anyone want some chocolate milk?" I asked. I had packed a lot of small chocolate milk drinks, and they were heavy to carry so I was hoping to get rid of some.

"I'll take one," Christoffer said.

I handed him one and looked at Ida. She was so pale. She looked like she was going to be sick. "Ida?"

She shook her head. I shrugged and opened one for myself. I was terrible at waiting like this. It was so boring. So I just kept eating. I found some chocolate and started on that as well. Sophia was soon moaning about her back. Carrying little baby Alma like this wore her out.

"Well, just a couple of hours more," I said with a smile.

Sophia laughed. "Well, that's hardly anything, now is it?"

The line moved a little bit and we moved ahead, too. I was about to pull out another piece of chocolate when suddenly I was interrupted by screaming up in the front of the line. Then someone was yelling in a megaphone really loud and the crowd ahead of us started screaming again. I stretched my neck to better see what was happening. The line had filled up behind us, but we were still among the ones in the back.

"Why are they screaming?" Christoffer asked.

I shrugged and stood on my tiptoes, but whatever was happening was too far away. "I don't know," I said. "But I would really like to find out."

Ida pulled my arm. Then she pointed into the sky. "Look," she said with a feeble voice.

I looked up and realized I had been staring in the wrong direction the entire time. Above our heads, a helicopter was slowly descending, and underneath it, on a small ladder, hung Patrick, holding the megaphone in his hand, yelling something. As he got closer, I could hear what it was he was yelling:

"Good morning, Fanoe! Are you ready to rrrrrumble?"

The crowd was screaming back.

"*Yes!*" and then started chanting his name. "*Patrick, Patrick, Patrick.*"

I laughed. "So typical him to make an entrance like that," I said. We all watched as the helicopter came closer to the ground. The screaming grew considerably in strength and volume. Patrick then let out one of his famous high-pitched screams that always made me think of Steven Tyler or Axl Rose.

I had to say, I loved it when he did that. There was no doubt the boy could definitely sing.

The crowd was screaming and clapping as Patrick came closer. Photographers from the magazines and papers were running around beneath him like small ants under a dinner table where sugar had been spilled on the floor, hoping to get that one shot that would hit the front cover the next day.

Now we could see him really close. The show's camera crew was filming everything. I started wondering where the helicopter was going to land. There wasn't enough room anywhere. Patrick had to come down here somehow, right?

Seconds later, I had my answer. A crew of people ran into the street and placed a huge inflatable thing. The helicopter descended further. Then Patrick waved at the crowd, pretended to not hold on, pretended that he missed the rope ladder when he tried to reach for it. The crowd screamed and gasped as he fell through the air, still screaming into the megaphone and landed on the inflatable. I held my breath, thinking he could hit all kinds of things on his way down or maybe even miss the inflatable and be smashed into the asphalt. But he didn't. Patrick jumped right out of the inflatable and lifted one arm into the air, giving the whole world the finger.

The crowd went berserk.

Patrick laughed and walked closer while the screaming increased. He ran to some of the girls behind a fence that marked the line and signed their books, arms, and chests. Then he held the megaphone to his mouth again.

"Do we have some Shooting Stars here today?" he yelled.

All the children screamed, "Yeeeeeess."

"Great. Let's get this party staaaaarted!"

The crowd clapped and screamed as Patrick ran from the beginning of the line down towards us in the back, giving high-fives to everybody on the way. Girls were crying hysterically. I leaned over the fence as he passed us and slapped him a high-five as well.

When he reached the back, he lifted the megaphone once again and yelled:

"Auditions are open!"

Then he was gone.

"Wow," I said with a huge smile. "Some showmanship, huh?"

Both of the children nodded eagerly.

"I want to be famous like Patrick," Christoffer said. "I should be famous."

Sophia laughed. Baby Alma still wasn't sleeping. Sophia's cheeks had turned red from all the rocking back and forth. I laughed too and messed up Christoffer's hair. "Well maybe you will be after today," I said, thinking it really had to be a special type of person who did what Patrick did. It wasn't something just anyone could do. I wondered what it was that had made Patrick such a huge celebrity. What was he even famous for doing? Being crazy? Hated by half of the population loved by the rest. It was hardly a career you would encourage your kid to pursue. But being famous for singing well wasn't a bad thing in my book. Still, I wasn't sure I wanted that kind of life for my kids. The life of a celebrity had to be rough. I wasn't so sure it was all fun like most kids believed. Luckily, neither of my kids seemed to want fame and stardom. And neither did I. I enjoyed my level of success immensely. Being a writer and having a bestselling book out now was great. I received letters every day from readers, but people still didn't recognize me on the street. In that way, I could continue to live my life as I always had.

"Emma?"

I turned to look for who had called my name. I spotted Officer Morten in the street. He was waving and walking closer.

"Hi there," I said. "How is everything? Busy day, huh?"

Officer Morten exhaled. "You wouldn't believe it. Not exactly another day at the office."

I chuckled. "You all alone here?"

"No, we've called for extra backup from the mainland. The place is packed with police officers. Dressed as civilians, most of them, but don't let that fool you. They all hope the bowtie killer will show his ugly face so they can finally take him down. They even came from a special homicide division in Copenhagen. Two guys who have been working on catching the killer for two years."

"Wow. Well at least that gets you off the hook," I said and smiled.

"I guess so. But I'm still going to be happier once this entire weekend is over and the show on Monday is done. I can't wait to get back to normal again."

"Guess you won't be complaining about it being too boring here again, huh?" I asked.

"Nope. Not for a long time."

"Any news about the Countess?" I asked.

"No. It's horrible. The press is all over the story. The royal family is going ballistic. Meanwhile, we have no idea where to look. It's like she has vanished completely from the face of the earth."

"Guess this is the time where the police would normally just say she had drowned, huh?" I said, thinking the statement was provocative, but not regretting being straightforward.

Officer Morten looked at me. "I guess you're right. If the same person who took Countess Josephine has taken all these other kids, then he is damn good at blurring his tracks. I still find it hard to believe, though, that this could have taken place for so many years without anyone connecting the dots."

I shrugged. "It is hard to believe, I'll give you that. Have you had time to look into the different cases to see if there any similarities?"

Officer Morten sighed. "A little bit. Not much. But there is one thing all the cases have in common, other than similarities in the victims."

The line was moving and I moved along with it. We were speaking with low voices, making sure no one else was able to hear our conversation.

"And what is that?"

"Well all of them—except Josephine's case, that is—were on the same playground when they were last seen."

"Really?"

"Yes. That's why the police concluded they were all drowning, because it's the playground down by Vesterhavsbad. Right by the beach. The conclusion is that they just ran off without their parents seeing, went into the water to try and go to the island, and then drowned."

"Josephine was taken from Vesterhavsbad too, wasn't she? That same beach?" I asked.

"That's what concerns me the most right now. Yes."

"So, do you think the kidnapper lives nearby or something?"

Officer Morten bit his lip. "Hardly. It's mostly summer cabins that tourists rent and we searched all of them looking for Josephine just the other day."

"Still, the kidnapper must have some connection to the area. He can't have walked far with Josephine, no?" I asked.

"Well, if he had a car nearby, he could."

"That's true."

Officer Morten received a phone call. "I have to go," he said. "I'm needed."

I nodded pensively. "Sure. Thanks for the info."

"Remember, this stays between you and me."

"Of course," I said, thinking about the book I had already started writing in my mind. Officer Morten was already walking away. I turned to face Sophia. Baby Alma had finally fallen asleep. Her face looked so relieved.

"What was that all about?" she asked, as we moved forward again.

I shook my head. "I'll tell you another day."

38

APRIL 2013

P atrick couldn't stop giggling. After the stunt outside, he had returned to his dressing room inside the old theater. Oh, what a joy. What a thrill to hear all those screaming voices calling his name, demanding his presence. Oh, how he loved it.

Now he was dancing around his room, twirling, wearing an old red cloak that he had found on the racks. It had probably been a part of some play.

Now it was going to be a part of his.

He looked at himself in the mirror while giggling, dancing, and just feeling high, ecstatic, slowly losing control.

Patrick, Patrick you can't lose it. You have to keep it together. Keep both feet on the ground!

"Shut up, you loser," Patrick hissed out loud to his own reflection. "I'll do whatever pleases me. And they'll love me for it. They'll love everything I do."

Don't do it, Patrick. Not on a day like this. Wait till it's all over like you usually do. They'll catch you. Someone will see...

"Didn't I tell you to shut the hell up? Nobody asked for your opinion, you pathetic little creature. You're not in charge anymore. I have wiped you out. I have cut you off. You're so weak. No one cares about you anymore."

Finally, his mind was quiet. Then he laughed again. His cheeks were blushing, probably from all the excitement. Patrick's hands were flickering in the air. He just couldn't...he could barely contain it anymore. He had to do it. He had to do something. It was just too...too tempting. With all the police everywhere...it was almost like they were challenging him. And Patrick loved a good challenge.

"I have to do it," he whispered. He licked his teeth in front of the mirror. "I simply have to," he hissed. "There's no use fighting it anymore."

Patrick found an old long-haired wig and put it on. He kept the cloak on, and put the hood up to cover his face. He put dark make-up on his eyes to make them look creepy before he left the dressing room.

The auditions always attracted a lot of strange people, dressing in weird costumes, so he blended in easily with the rest of the crowd. He wasn't supposed to be on for at least an hour, so he had plenty of time to do his little thing. As he walked along the corridors of the theater, he felt a thrill race through his entire body. The anticipation of finally getting his fix. The excitement of the danger of getting caught. It was so...so alluring, so arousing.

Patrick felt the butterfly-knife in his pants underneath the cloak. This was going to be so much fun.

Patrick didn't have to walk long before he found his victim. She was standing in front of the toilets behind the scenes where the auditions were. It was a secluded area for people who worked on the show or people who were done with their auditions. But they usually left quickly, for the most part.

She wasn't old, but Patrick had been looking to go younger for a while. He hated those more than anything. The small girls who were oh, so pretty, oh, so adorable with their long hair and sparkling eyes. To him, they were the ultimate victims. So innocent, not yet corrupted by the world and all its evil. They had not yet experienced the roughness of life, the harshness of people.

He wanted to be the one to introduce them to that. That was the plan. To ruin their innocence, spoil the feeling of security that they still possessed, the belief that the world was a nice place and that people were good. This girl seemed to still posses all of that.

"Hi there," Patrick said.

The girl looked into his eyes. "You're Patrick, aren't you?" she asked.

"Yes. And you're a smart girl, aren't you? What are you doing back here all alone?"

"I was just in the bathroom. I'm waiting for my mom. She told me to wait for her outside."

"She's in there?" Patrick asked with a shrill edge to his voice.

"Yes. I've just done my audition and we're going home afterwards."

No, you're not!

"I see. Did you go through to the next round? Did you DAZZLE the judges? Did you make them just LOOVE you?"

The girl looked at him. He smiled. Then she shook her head. "Ah, that's too bad. I'm sure they made the wrong decision. I'm sure you're absolutely FABOULOUS."

The girl was shy and looked down. "I don't know..."

"Oh, but I do. I might know a way for you to get in anyway. Would you be interested in that?"

The girl looked up, then nodded heavily. A sparkle of hope was lit in her eyes.

"Okay then," Patrick said with a grin. "Come with me."

"But...but what about my mom?" she asked.

"Don't worry about her. I'll have someone tell her where you are when she gets out. Don't worry. She'll be very pleased that you did this. You'll be FAMOUS after this. I'll put you on the cover of all the papers. Just you wait and see."

"I'd like that," she said, and put her small hand in his. "I'd really like that."

39

AUGUST 2004

"**I** want both of them."

The man who pointed at Nina and Blanka next to her was sweating heavily. He wiped his forehead with a handkerchief. His hair was greasy, his hands and arms covered in black hair. *Looks like a monkey*, Nina thought to herself.

He had been in there before, but never picked Nina. She felt good that he finally picked her. The man was important; she had learned that much. Nadja, the woman who took care of the place always acted different when he was there. Now she smiled and nodded. He was a mafia boss, Blanka had told Nina. He was the one who owned the brothel that Nina had been brought to two years ago when she was last sold. Now she was closer to town. Which town, she didn't know, but some town. She watched the beautiful lights at night and dreamed herself away.

"Nina and Blanka, go with Mr. Zaleski," Nadja said. She

grabbed Nina's arm as she passed her. "Now, don't let me down. Do everything he says. Make him happy and you make me happy, okay? You'll get reward. Big reward."

"Like what?" Nina asked. She had been in this business for a long time now, and knew that she was worth a lot of money. She was the only one who could speak to Nadja in this way.

"Food. I'll give you steak, you like steak, huh?"

Nina shook her head. "Not enough. I want something else."

Nadja sighed. "Okay, no men for two days. Make Mr. Zaleski happy and you'll be off for two whole days. You stay in your room, but you don't work, alright?"

"Blanka, too," Nina said. "She gets reward, too."

Nadja closed her eyes. "Okay. Blanka, too. But just go before he changes his mind. Remember. Make him happy."

Nina smiled as she grabbed Blanka's hand and walked towards her room. She looked at Blanka before they walked inside with the greasy man. Then she winked at her to let her know about the reward.

"No men for two days," she whispered.

Blanka's eyes glistened with joy. Nina looked at her and felt great love for her. She had loved Blanka from the first day she came to the brothel. It was almost a year ago and what a year it had been. Blanka was young, much younger than she, and Nina had taken it upon herself to take care of her, explain to her how things worked around there. Blanka had thought she was going away for a job at a restaurant in Greece to support her family back in Slovakia, where they were suffering badly. She was no more than fourteen when they sent her away to work and send back money. But they were tricked, as was Blanka. She never went to Greece; instead, she was brought to the same brothel as Nina. She had never even been with a man before she came there, and now she had been molested by hundreds already. Nina felt bad for her and had taken good care of her, as good as she possibly could, given their circumstances. But she could never protect her from all the bad things, and that hurt her so deeply. At least now that the man had picked the both of them, Nina could make sure he didn't hurt Blanka. She could keep Blanka away from all the nasty stuff and make sure he only did it to her. In Nina's eyes, Blanka was as pure as snow. In fact, she was certain that she loved her deeply. Nina had never loved anyone before, and it felt strange and absurd, but at the same time so right. Blanka was so right. Her skin like caramel, her eyes brown as almonds, her hair smooth as silk.

"Now, you two kiss," the nasty man said while sitting on the bed.

Nina smiled and looked at Blanka, who smiled back. Yes, Nina was certain Blanka loved her as well, and the thought of kissing her instead of that old ugly man was quite compelling. Nina leaned over and closed her eyes. The kiss was soft and tasted sweet. Nina's heart was beating fast in her chest.

"No, no," the man yelled. "With tongue. Like this," he said and stuck out his tongue. "Like that."

Nina shrugged, then leaned over and grabbed Blanka's face between her hands. She closed her eyes again as she opened her mouth and kissed the only person she had ever loved on this cruel earth.

40

———————

APRIL 2013

"**I**DA? **W**HERE IS **I**DA?"

Sophia looked at me nervously. I was standing by the door leading to the scene where Christoffer was auditioning right now. I couldn't hear much, but by the look on the judges' faces through the glass window, he shouldn't count on becoming famous any time soon.

"Have you seen Ida?" Sophia asked again.

I shook my head. "I thought she was with you."

"She was. We went to the bathroom together and I asked her to wait for me outside. I had to change Alma's diaper. When I came out, she was gone."

"Do you think she might have gotten lost?" I asked. "There's a lot of corridors down there. It's an old theater where the actors were supposed to be able to get on stage from all kinds of places, probably even from under the stage."

Sophia nodded. "I guess she might be lost. Maybe I should go look for her?"

"Do that. I'll wait here for Christoffer. He should be done soon," I said.

I watched Sophia disappear down a corridor, calling Ida's name. I turned my head and looked at Christoffer, secretly hoping to catch a glimpse of Patrick, but he didn't seem to be in there with the judges.

"Well, hello there. How's it going?"

The voice was coming from behind me and could come from none other than Patrick himself. I turned and looked at him. For some reason, I blushed. "I think it's going pretty good," I lied.

Patrick's eyes flickered maniacally. I had never seen him this close in real life and never noticed that look on him before. It was a little creepy, like he was about to lose it and have a manic breakdown or something. I don't know what it was.

"So, you're his mom?" Patrick asked and peeked in through the window, as well.

I stepped backwards to let him see better. He was wearing a long red cloak and a wig. I figured it was all a part of his weird act, but there didn't seem to be any cameras around. Maybe he was just always acting.

"No, I'm his neighbor. His mom just went out to find his sister."

"So, he has a sister too, huh? Does she sing?"

"She does. But right now we're afraid she might have gotten lost in the corridors of the theater."

Patrick turned his head fast, almost like an owl, and looked at me. His right eye had a tick in it. "Oh? Is that so?" he said. "Well, I do hope nothing bad has happened to her down there."

I wrinkled my forehead. "What do you mean? What bad could happen? We're in a theater and the place is packed with police."

"No. No. Of course not. Of course she's fine. I just meant that maybe she would be all AFRAID or something."

Patrick yelled the word very loud it made me jump. He was even weirder in person, it seemed. I had always thought it was just an act, but now I realized that it was just the way he was.

"Well, I think she'll be fine," I said, and hoped Christoffer would be done soon so I could get away from this lunatic. I was highly uncomfortable in his presence. If he wasn't a famous TV host, I think he would have been locked up somewhere and had the key thrown away. Or, at the very least, be highly medicated.

"Of COURSE she will," he yelled. "She's fine. She's just FINE."

Patrick breathed heavily and looked at me while his right eye kept blinking constantly. I think he saw that I noticed because he put on his sunglasses really fast. Then he smiled awkwardly. "Hot today, huh?"

It really wasn't. It was one of those icy cold days where the wind blew in from the North Sea, but I didn't want to tell him that. I was very disappointed and just wanted to go home.

I looked at him with a strange feeling that he wasn't really well, when suddenly we were interrupted by an ear piercing scream that made me forget everything. It was coming from the corridors. My heart literally stopped and everything inside of me froze. I knew that voice.

It was Sophia.

41

AUGUST 2004

Their lips parted and Nina opened her eyes. She immediately felt remorse for letting go of Blanka's lips. It was like being torn in half. Nina wanted the kiss to last longer, she wanted them to stay this close forever. Just the two of them forgetting everything around them, forgetting about the fat sweaty man who was breathing heavily on the bed now, forgetting that they were trapped in this place, in this prison of hell. Forgetting the world with all its strange desires and unpleasantries.

"Yeah, that's the stuff. Now, you touch her breast, bite her nipple," the man said to Nina. He had taken his pants off and was holding his *thing* in his hand.

Nina looked at Blanka, looked into her deep brown eyes where she knew she could escape, swim deep into them like an ocean and forget everything else, just shut out the cruelties of the world. In there, in those deep brown eyes, was salvation.

There Nina found the safe haven that she had been longing for...for so desperately long.

Nina lifted her hand and stroke Blanka's cheek gently. Then she grabbed her tiny breast in her hand, cupped it, and held it for a little while. Blanka gasped. Nina smiled and leaned over to kiss her again, dreaming about those soft lips touching hers once again, but the sweaty man interrupted them.

"No kissing. Biting," he said, and snapped his teeth. "Bite the nipple."

Nina looked at Blanka again. She was still holding her breast in her one hand like it was the most important treasure in the world. Blanka smiled. Nina smiled back. Then she leaned over and put Blanka's breast in her mouth.

"Yeah. Yeah. That's it," the man yelled while touching himself. "That's the stuff I like. Now bite the nipple. Bite it."

Nina let her tongue caress the nipple gently and closed her eyes, listening to the beating of Blanka's heart. Carefully, she bit the nipple gently. Blanka gasped and moaned. Nina breathed heavily as she sucked on it and then on the other one, nipping on them, letting them fill her mouth and tasting the sweet drops of sweat on Blanka's skin.

"Yeah. Yeah. That's it."

The man kept going, but the girls didn't hear him anymore, they hardly even sensed his presence in the room any longer. It was like he wasn't important anymore. Soon, he became like a distant figure that had no relevance to the two of them. Nina simply didn't care about him anymore. She had finally figured out where she belonged in this forsaken and evil world. For the first time in her almost fifteen years of living, she felt like she belonged. She had finally come home.

But it didn't last many minutes before she was pulled out of it and back to the harsh reality of her miserable life. As she was kissing Blanka's soft skin on her stomach, she was pulled out of her hands, ripped from her place of safety.

The man had gotten up from the bed and grabbed Blanka around the waist. He pulled her towards the bed and threw her on top of it. Blanka whimpered with fear.

"No," Nina said. Her heart racing in her chest. "Take me instead. She is too young. I have experience."

The man walked over to Nina and hammered his fist into her face. Nina fell backwards onto the floor, her nose bleeding heavily. The room was spinning as she was trying to figure out what was up and what was down. She heard Blanka cry and as Nina regained her sight and was able to focus again, she saw Blanka bent over the bed. Next the man leaned down to the floor and found his socks. He rolled them into a small ball that he stuffed into Blanka's mouth. She was crying and whimpering, looking at Nina for help as he grabbed her around the waist and forced her to bend over further. Tears were rolling down her cheeks and the socks in her mouth forced her to fight to breathe. Furthermore, the man held a hand across her face so she couldn't open her mouth and she could hardly breathe through her nose either, because of her crying. Nina watched Blanka with anxiousness as fear rolled across her eyes while she was fighting to breathe. Blanka was trying to scream, but ended up gagging. Soon, she started choking. Nina cried, worrying about the man hurting Blanka. She got up on her feet and walked towards them.

"Stop," Nina whispered. Then she repeated it a little louder. "You have to stop."

The man didn't react.

Nina could tell by the look on Blanka's face that she was in deep pain. That was when she realized that Blanka had thrown up.

"She's choking. You have to stop. She's choking!" Nina suddenly yelled.

But it was too late. Nina watched Blanka's eyes roll back in her head and she lost consciousness.

"Stop!" Nina yelled again and ran to help Blanka. She tried to remove the fingers from Blanka's face to ease her breathing, so she could cough up the vomit before it blocked her throat completely and suffocated her. But the man lifted his hand and slapped her so hard Nina fell backwards and down from the bed.

Before Nina managed to get back on her feet, the man finally let her go, but Blanka still didn't move. Nina ran to Blanka and opened her mouth. She reached down in her throat and pulled out the socks that blocked her breathing, but it was too late. Nina felt for a pulse, but there was none.

Blanka was dead.

42

APRIL 2013

I ran as fast as I could down the corridor, followed by Patrick and another guy who had heard the scream also.

We found Sophia standing in front of an open door. She had both of her hands to her face and an open mouth. When I got to her, she was still screaming. My heart was beating fast now while a million thoughts ran through my mind.

Is it Ida? Has something happened to Ida? Please, don't let it be her. Please, let it be something else. Let it be a huge rat or something. Not Ida.

I put my arm on Sophia's shoulder and she stopped screaming. "What's going on? What happened?" As I spoke, I turned my head and looked inside the room that Sophia was still staring into. Patrick did the same. Then he started screaming as well, holding his hands to his face.

"Oh, my God," he said, cupping his mouth. "Oh, my God."

"The door was open," Sophia said sobbing. "I looked in and found this, found her sitting like that."

I gasped as I realized what it was Sophia had seen. A small girl was sitting inside the room on a chair, her head hanging to the side, her eyes staring blankly into the empty air. Underneath her chair was a huge pool of blood that had run down from the chair. The lights in the room were on and turned towards her like spotlights on stage. Like she was on display, like the killer wanted us to see her.

"It's not Ida," I said. "It's not Ida." I wasn't proud of it, but a big part of me was so relieved that it wasn't her, but some other girl. I calmed my breathing and tried to think fast. That was when I noticed the bowtie. It was sewn onto her chest, since the girl wasn't old enough to have developed breasts yet. It made me feel sick. Who would hurt such a young innocent girl? What kind of sick bastard would do something like this?

"The police. We need to alert the police. They're outside with all the contestants by the waiting room. I'll run out to them," I said.

"I'll go with you," Patrick said, and started walking next to me. The third person who had run to the scene put his arm around Sophia and helped her sit down on a cardboard box next to them.

We ran through the corridor, and not far from the scene, I suddenly spotted Ida walking towards us.

"What's going on?"

"Ida!" I yelled and grabbed her in my arms.

"What's going on?" she repeated.

"I thought...for one small second there I was so scared that..."

I inhaled deeply, then looked into Ida's eyes. "Something bad happened back there. I want you to walk with me. I don't want you to see it. Maybe you could go back and be there when your brother comes out of his audition. He's probably done by now. Could you do that for me?"

Ida looked at Patrick in his red cloak. He smiled at her and she smiled back. "Okay. I can do that."

"Great. I'll be right back."

I grabbed Patrick's arm and pulled him with me towards the waiting area. The crowd started screaming when they spotted Patrick with me, but he didn't seem to notice. He seemed perplexed and out of it. I spotted Officer Morten right away and ran towards him. Patrick followed me.

"We have a situation in the back," I said. "It's bad. It's really bad."

Officer Morten became serious. "Is it...?

I exhaled deeply. "Yes. I'm afraid it is. And it's a child this time. A little girl." It hurt like swallowing knives to say it out loud.

Patrick seemed pretty out of it and was whimpering and walking in circles as I spoke to the officer. "Oh, man," he said biting his nails. "She had a bowtie...right here," he said and pointed at his chest.

"Let's go," Officer Morten said. "Show me the way."

43

APRIL 2013

It was the most fun Patrick had ever had. And it was all his own doing.

You only have the fun you create yourself. Life is what you make of it. If you get lemons, then...well, then don't worry about it, just have your fun anyway. Try to stab someone, see the blood running, feel the power of life and death in your hands. That'll make you forget everything else.

He wanted so badly to laugh out loud and jump around in exaltation, but he restrained himself. He had to continue to play out his act. It was all part of the show. He had to stay in character. And he was so believable it was almost frightening. Not a soul suspected a thing. He was as upset and troubled about this as anyone. Maybe even more than most people. Producer Hanne had heard about it and was now holding his hand as he was sitting on a chair in the corridor, crying his heart out, letting her know how absolutely *awful* this all was. How terrified he was that people could be so *evil*, so *cruel*.

"She was only a little girl," he said, holding a hand theatrically to his chest. Hanne patted him on his shoulder.

From the corner of his eye, Patrick watched as the police worked the scene. He recognized the officers who had been to his suite the day before, Nyberg and Gammelgaard. They seemed troubled and concerned. Their faces so deadly serious. Patrick enjoyed watching them immensely. He could hardly believe that this was all his work. And what a work indeed.

Beautiful, Patrick. Your best one yet. And the lights? The girl killed on her search for fame, put in the spotlight for the entire world to see. Making her more famous that she would ever have been on her own? Genius. It's as simple as that. The work of a mastermind. Some might even say you did her a favor. You fulfilled her dream in death. Astonishing. You've outdone yourself this time.

"Do you want to go back to the hotel and rest a little?" Hanne said, looking at her watch. "We'll have to take a break here anyway, probably for the rest of the day till the police are done examining the room." Hanne sighed and cursed. "Bloody day to choose to kill someone. We're losing a lot of money here, people. Lots of money."

Patrick hid his face in between his hands and peered out inconspicuously between his fingers. He spotted the woman sitting not too far away. She was the one who had been waiting outside the door when they heard the scream. There was something about her that made him want to watch her. She wasn't pretty in the way his many victims had been. But she had a beautiful face, and that annoyed him immensely. She was comforting the other woman, the one that had found the body, while talking to a police officer. He was taking her statement and writing down what she said.

"I think I need to talk to the police first," Patrick said. They told anyone who was at the scene when the body was found to stay. Afterwards, I would love to go back to the hotel and rest."

"Alright," Hanne said with a yawn. "I'll take you then." She looked at her watch again, then pulled out her phone and started tapping on it. Then she sighed. "Okay. Now it's official. They've called off the auditions for today. We'll just have to take the rest tomorrow. It's gonna be one hell of a long day. Better be ready for that, darling."

Patrick nodded. "I'm ready," he said. "Ain't no killer gonna stop me from doing what I love to do. The show must go on, right?"

Hanne laughed. It seemed delightfully inappropriate, given the circumstances. Patrick liked that. He wanted to laugh too, but he had the decency to stay in character. That was what made him a good actor, a great showman. He never lost his cool. Not in public, at least.

"That's my Patrick," she said. "That's what I like to hear."

44

AUGUST 2004

Nina stared at the sweaty man as he looked at her, thirsty with lust.

"So, now you and me, alright? Come over here."

Nina exhaled sharply. "She's...she's...she's dead. You killed her." Her voice was quavering, her heart was beating fast now, and she felt sick to her stomach. She could hardly believe this was happening. How could this be happening? Now? When she had finally found someone...someone to love, when she was finally starting to believe that there was something nice in this world again, that somewhere there was a place for her in all this evil, all this malice that she was surrounded by.

And, just like that, it was gone? Just like that, *she* was gone? How? Why? Why did this world insist on putting her down in the dirt?

Nina felt how the anger arose inside of her, causing her blood to boil. She could hardly hear what the man was saying anymore. The blood rushing through her veins was drowning out everything else.

The man leaned over and felt Blanka's pulse. Just the thought of him touching her fragile skin once again made Nina see red. It was like her entire view was blurred by blood, and the strong desire to see this man bleed and suffer the same horrors her beloved had.

He didn't find a pulse, then let Blanka's hand fall flaccid back on the bed. Then he shrugged. He looked at Nina lustfully, then licked his lips, letting his tongue caress the black hairs on his upper lip.

"Too bad," he said. "Such a pretty girl."

That was when Nina finally lost it. In one great leap, she jumped the man and sat on his shoulders. She screamed like a wild animal before she bent down and bit into his ear. The man screamed and tried to pull her down, but Nina burrowed her long nails that Nadja made sure all the girls had and took care of, into his skin. Blood was gushing out from the ear and the pierced skin, running down his face and shoulders. The sweaty man was groaning while turning and trying to throw Nina off, but she held on, while scratching and biting him like a crazed wild animal. She bit so hard into his ear that soon a big chunk of it came loose and she spat it out onto the floor. The man screamed in anger and pain. He grabbed Nina by the leg and finally managed to pull her off his back. He threw her through the air and she landed on her back onto a dresser. It hurt like hell, but Nina was so angry she didn't care. No amount of physical pain could ever measure up to the emotional pain Nina was going through right now. And that gave her the strength to do what she did next.

The man was stunned, but steaming with anger, and he walked toward her with his fists clenched. She tried to get up on her feet, but her hand slipped on the floor, reaching in under the dresser where it touched a shoe. All the shoes they were provided in the brothel looked the same, so she didn't have to look at it to know it was a high heeled stiletto shoe. Just as the man came close enough, Nina pulled it out from under the dresser and hit the heel into the man's right eye. As it struck his eye, she realized it had gone so deep she couldn't move it. She let go and the man screamed and fell to the ground, trying to pull the heel out of his heavily bleeding eye. Nina got up and walked over to him and kicked him in the crotch. Then she leaned over and grabbed the shoe again. She put her foot on his face and pulled the heel out of his eye. The man hollered in pain and blood spurted out of the eye that had been so badly damaged it no longer resembled an eye, just a blob of bloody jelly.

Nina waited a few seconds until the man once again looked at her with his remaining good eye. She waited because she wanted to look into it when she did the next thing. She wanted to see his fear, to watch the terror in his one eye when he realized what she was about to do. Then, she smashed the heel into his other eye and blinded him completely.

45

APRIL 2013

Sophia was still in shock when we entered my house later that afternoon. And I guess so was I. Christoffer and Ida were quiet all the way home and not once did I hear them discuss the auditions. Christoffer hadn't gone through to the next round, but Ida had. Under normal circumstances, it would be something to celebrate.

I opened the door and let the kids and Sophia in. My dad came out and hugged me. I had called him from the theater to let him know what was going on and why we were going to be very late.

"How are you doing?" he asked.

That was when I finally broke down and cried. After hours of keeping my cool, I couldn't hold it in any longer. It had to come out somehow. My dad held me tight and helped me into the kitchen, so the kids wouldn't see me cry. Sophia was soon surrounded by her children, who all wanted something from her. They dragged her into the living room while I was alone with my dad.

"That bad, huh?" he asked. "I've made coffee. Do you want some?"

I nodded, while making sobbing sounds. "I can't believe it, Dad. I mean she was just a little girl. No more than nine years old. Who would do something so horrible like that?"

My dad shook his head heavily. "I don't know, sweetie. I wish I had some answer to make you feel better, but I really don't."

"For a moment, I thought it was Ida. I was so scared, Dad. I could hardly bear it." I sniffled and my dad handed me a tissue.

"I think this calls for one of these," my dad said, and placed a small chocolate turtle in front of me. They were my favorites and always had been since I was a child.

I chuckled while sobbing still. "Thanks, Dad. I think you're right."

I felt slightly better after eating it, not so much because of the chocolate, but because of my dad's concern for me. He'd always had a way of comforting me when I was sad, and he could still do it. "I can't believe you remembered how much I loved these," I said, while chewing on the turtle. The cream inside of it melted on my tongue.

"How could I forget?" he said, and poured me a second cup of coffee.

It felt nice to sit in the kitchen with my dad again and just sip coffee and not have to say anything.

After a few minutes, Helle peeked in. "How are you doing?" she said.

"Okay, I guess. You heard what happened?"

"Your dad told me and I heard some on the radio, too."

"On the radio?" I asked. "I thought you were here all afternoon?"

She shook her head. "No, I went to the shop for a little while just to check in on Jack. He's been down there all day painting. It's going really well."

"So, you were downtown when this happened?" I said, thinking about the bowties. I wasn't sure where I was going with this. It was absurd.

My dad looked at me like I was crazy. I felt like I was, but couldn't escape the thought. She was the only one that I had seen with access to bowties like the ones I had seen sewn onto the victim's chests. I shook my head and sipped my coffee. No, it was stupid. I was just jealous because she was my dad's new girlfriend. That was all it was.

"Horrible thing about that girl who has gone missing too, huh?" she said. "She was a Countess, I've read."

"Was?" I asked. "As far as I know, she's not dead yet."

Helle shrugged. "No. It's just a long time already since she went missing, so I assumed that she might...Do you think it might be the same killer? Do you think the bowtie killer took her as well, then killed her, but they just haven't found the body yet?"

I sighed and sipped more coffee while thinking it through. It was the easiest explanation to all of this, but I didn't buy it.

46

APRIL 2013

I didn't sleep much that night. I kept tossing and turning, seeing that poor girl in front of my eyes, crying for her and her poor family. Around three in the morning, I went downstairs to get a glass of milk. I peeked inside first Maya's room to make sure she was alright, then inside Victor's. Maya was sleeping heavily, whereas Victor seemed to be sleeping uneasily. He was tossing and moaning in his bed, and the sheets and blanket were all knotted up around him. I walked closer and put my hand on top of his head carefully and started patting him, in the hope that it would make him calm down. His face was strained and he was sweating. I wondered if he was coming down with a fever.

"Shh," I hushed, as I stroked his hair gently. It felt great to be able to touch him again. I missed so much holding him in my arms. I quietly cried, thinking about the young girl at the theater. Her mother was never going to hold her again, never going to see her grow up, never going to hear her sing again.

Victor was calmer now. His face still seemed stressed, like he was struggling in his sleep, but he had stopped tossing. I was filled with an overwhelming gratefulness that he was still in my life.

"I love you so much, Victor," I whispered.

I leaned over him and kissed his cheek with my eyes closed. When I opened them again and leaned back, Victor was suddenly moving. He opened his eyes and looked directly at me. I pulled back with a gasp.

"Sorry if I woke you, buddy," I said.

But Victor didn't react. His eyes were looking at me, but he didn't seem to see me at all. "What's wrong? Did you have a bad dream or something?"

Victor didn't answer. He sat up. It was starting to get a little creepy. The way he moved, the way his eyes looked made him look just like a doll. Like a human sized doll. It kind of reminded me of the dolls I had seen in Helle's store. I stepped backwards. Victor turned his head like an owl and stared directly at me. His eyes were glasslike and hardly looked real. His upper body and arms were stiff as he moved them. He lifted his right arm, which was bent at a ninety-degree angle, and put his pointer finger to his lips, signaling for me to be quiet.

Moving almost like a robot—or a doll—he took his arm down, then leaned back into the bed. As soon as his head hit the pillow, his eyelids closed. He fell back to sleep with his arms still pointing up in the air. My heart was racing heavily as I watched him doze off and his body turn back to normal again. His arms soon relaxed and fell to the bed, his head turned to the side on the pillow, and as suddenly as it had appeared, the stiffness in his body was completely gone.

I blinked several times and kept staring at him for at least ten minutes more before I dared move. I couldn't believe what I had seen. Could I have been dreaming? Hallucinating from lack of sleep? From the stress and shock I had been through the last couple of days?

I listened to his steady breathing, and as soon as I was certain he was sleeping heavily again, I sneaked back out into the hallway. I went downstairs, taking deep breaths trying to calm myself down. I grabbed a glass and filled it with milk from the refrigerator. I drank it, but it didn't make me any calmer. I kept wondering about what I had seen. What did it mean? Was he just dreaming? He had been right about the bowtie this week and the spiders last year. What did the doll mean? Did it have something to do with my dad's new girlfriend, Helle? If so, then what?

I rubbed my head and suddenly felt so confused by every-thing. I kept thinking about that girl, Josephine Gyldenstjerne, who had gone missing this week. Could Helle be right? Was she just another one of the bowtie killer's victims? But what about the other children that had gone missing earlier then?

I went to my laptop in the living room and opened it. I found the old articles written about the first children to have disappeared. The first one was a six-year-old girl named Nina Kristensen. She had been playing on the playground when her mother had lost track of her. She'd looked all over, but couldn't find her daughter. All they found was the girl's doll on the ground.

Doll? I thought and looked up from the screen. It was still pitch dark outside. The wind had picked up in the trees and I could hear the branches scrape against the roof of my house. *Could that just be a coincidence? Was that what Victor was trying to tell me? Was there a connection between the dolls and the missing girls?*

I searched the rest of the articles about the other girls that had gone missing, but there was nothing about dolls in them. So that couldn't be it. There had to be something else. I found the first article again and saw the picture of Nina Kristensen's doll. It was dirty and had one eye broken. *Little Miss Jasmine*, it said underneath. It didn't look like the dolls in Helle's store. They looked more like real children, which was what made them so creepy. They all had long thick hair, this one didn't. Little Miss Jasmine was more like a baby doll. But there was one thing about it that once again made me think about Helle.

There was a big bowtie on the bottom part of the dress.

47

JANUARY 2005

She had escaped her prison just to enter a new one. After blinding the sweaty mafia boss at the brothel six months ago, Nina had thought she was going to be killed by Nadja's many security guys that kept beating the girls up and raping them as they pleased. But luck had been on her side on that terrifying day.

When Nina had still been in the room and watched with pleasure how the mafia boss squirmed on the floor in utter pain, she had noticed a big knife attached to his ankle. She had pulled it out while the man was still screaming. For a second, she had considered killing him on the spot, releasing him from his pain, but quickly she decided that would be letting him off the hook too easily. She liked the idea of him having to go through life without being able to see again, crippled and having to depend on the mercy of others.

Nina smiled and steeled herself for what was going to

happen next. She placed herself right at the door opening, so as soon as it opened and Nadja stormed in to see what the screaming was all about, Nina plunged the knife deep into her stomach. It took Nadja by such a surprise, she hardly realized what had happened until it was too late. She fell to the ground, blood spurting out of her mouth and stomach, coloring the floor red, and landed next to the squirming mafia boss with a thud.

It was almost too easy, Nina thought, as she pulled the knife out and stabbed Nadja again. Nina was a little disappointed that she died so fast. She would have liked to see her suffer, and she wanted to make sure she knew who had done this to her, who was the cause of her suffering. But now it was too late. She was already dead. Nina pulled the knife out of her chest and stabbed Nadja again and again. Nina was panting and sweating now, as she kept poking more holes in the already dead woman. It was almost as if she couldn't stop. She wanted to keep stabbing her, punishing her for all she had done. For all the years lost, for all the months and days she had kept her in this place, for all the time she had held her prisoner. For the many long merciless nights with one man after another.

Nina soon stopped herself. She had to get moving if she was going to survive this. Quickly, she cut Nadja's skirt open and found the small gun she knew she had attached to her leg. She pulled it out, then left the room holding it up in front of her. She ran down the hallway to Nadja's room, where she found clothes she could wear for her escape. Nina soon heard voices and footsteps in the hallway and figured the guards had realized what had happened. There was knocking on doors all the way down the hallway and girls were screaming.

Usually, Nina would be scared to death of these sounds, but not anymore. Nina had nothing to lose now. She grabbed the gun and went into the hallway. As soon as the first guard spotted her, she lifted up the gun and shot him between the eyes. His eyes rolled back and he fell backwards on the wooden planks with a loud bump. Nina breathed heavily and closed her eyes for just a second. She wanted to savor this moment of utter power, unlike anything she had ever experienced in her young life. For once, she was the one taking lives, she was the one deciding who was to live and who wasn't.

Another guard yelled and ran towards her. *That poor sucker.* He'd barely lifted his gun before Nina had shot him in the face, killing him instantly. Then she turned, and as another guard lifted his gun with the intention of shooting her in the back, she shot him as well. Then she bent down and grabbed one of the guard's guns and started walking downstairs, holding guns in both of her hands, feeling more powerful and alive than ever in her life.

If anything moved, she shot. There was no mercy; she didn't stop and ask. Dressed in Nadja's expensive clothes, she walked through the hall downstairs that she had been in so many times dancing for the dirty old men, glancing at the door in the distance with the exit sign above it, dreaming for what was on the other side. Longing to be able to once again walk outside and breathe in the fresh air. To be able to go wherever she wanted to.

Nina took in a deep breath and didn't look back before she grabbed the handle and turned the lock. She heard so much screaming behind her as the door closed and she was finally,

finally on the other side, the big mysterious outside, standing in the street among ordinary people walking by the house of terror that had kept her prisoner for years, like it was any other ordinary house that they never cared about and never would.

A woman gasped and crossed the street when she saw Nina with her guns, and Nina realized that from now on it was all about laying low. She put the guns in the pockets of her jacket, then started walking along the street, not knowing what day or even what year it was. And, worst of all, without knowing where to go.

Nina walked for hours with the sole purpose of getting as far away from the brothel as possible. But she wasn't wearing enough clothes, and soon she was freezing. She considered using the guns to rob a convenience store or maybe just some poor sucker on the street, but the last thing she wanted was to be found by the Polish police. She knew what happened to women like her. They would rape her and sell her to a new pimp. That was what the other girls at the brothel told her, and she stuck to what she knew.

By the time it was getting dark, Nina found herself outside of an old bakery looking in at all the food, feeling hunger eating her up from the inside.

That was when a big black car drove up next to her and the windows were rolled down. A man stuck his head out.

"How much?" he asked.

Nina swallowed hard to try and drown the little pride she had left. She approached the window and looked in.

"Five hundred," she said with a small voice. *Just enough to get me out of here*, she thought, and jumped inside the car as the door was opened. It was dangerous to get into a car like this. She had heard many stories of women being abused and tortured mercilessly by rich guys like this one, but Nina wasn't afraid of him. She reached down and felt the guns in her pockets. No one could touch her anymore.

The man brought her to his home, a beautiful mansion outside of town, where he kept her for days, paying her for every day he wanted her to stay. Much to Nina's surprise, he didn't hurt her on the first night and not on the second one, either. He wanted to do all the same stuff as most of the other men, but he didn't beat her afterwards or threaten her. All he wanted was for her to stay at his house, he said. She was to stay in one part of the mansion and never leave until he told her she could. Someone brought her three meals a day. She had to eat them in her room, but they were good meals of fresh meat and vegetables, and even cake and cookies for dessert. He was gone most of the day, but at night he entered her chambers and had sex with her. Then he left, putting more money on the counter for her. After a week, Nina had saved a lot of money, enough to get by for a long time. But the man wasn't done with her yet, he said.

"I want you to stay one more night," he kept telling her. And so she did. One more night became a week, a week became a month and now she had been there for almost six months at his house.

Nina dressed herself in clothes the man bought for her, a new dress almost every day, and jewelry that he told her she could keep. Nina couldn't believe her own ears or eyes for that matter. In just six months, she had blossomed into a woman. She had gained a lot of weight from all the food his servants brought her during the day. And she was now dressed like one of the rich ladies that the other girls at the brothel had told her about. She didn't mind him dressing her up like a doll, even though it did remind her of her mother.

Some nights he would just look at her and sometimes he even just wanted to brush her hair all night. Nina let him, even though she herself loathed every second of it.

"Why can't I leave the house?" she asked one night when he came to her chambers carrying a very expensive designer dress in his hands.

"Because I don't want you to," he answered firmly.

"But I want to take a stroll in the garden. I want to be able to breathe fresh air," Nina said. ·

"Then open the windows."

"I want to be able to walk, to dance in the yard, to look up at the blue sky. I want to be able to go into town. Can't I go into town, please?"

"You'll get dirty in the yard," he said with a smile. "And the city is no place for a beautiful girl like you." Then he leaned over and whispered in her ear the words he would come to regret. *"Baby doll."*

Nina saw red. How she loathed these two words more than anything in the world. Memories of her mother calling her those exact two words when she dressed her in those awful dresses and brushed her hair appeared in her head and poisoned her mind with unsustainable furor.

Nina pulled away, and found the mafia boss's old knife that she had hidden under her pillow in case she needed it one day. She pulled it out and stabbed him in the chest. The man stared at her in astonishment and held a hand to the knife. Blood was gushing out of his mouth as he fell backwards to the bed. Nina stared at him, and much to her surprise, she felt no pity, no mercy. Not even for the one man who had ever treated her nicely. No, in fact, she realized she enjoyed watching him die slowly and painfully looking up at her like he wanted her to somehow rescue him or at least explain herself.

As soon as he was dead, she gathered all her jewelry and some of her expensive dresses and dragged out two big suitcases she found in a closet. Then she threw in anything valuable that she could fit in the suitcases and emptied the man's pockets of his wallet and cash. She even stripped him of his expensive looking watch and diamante rings. Also his golden necklace that she had stared at so many times with him on top of her, speculating how much it was worth. She filled the suitcases till they could barely close, then ran downstairs to the servants that had been bringing her food.

"I need a car to take me to town," she said, with as much authority as her fifteen-year-old voice could muster. "Now."

48

APRIL 2013

They moved the rest of the auditions to an old movie theater on the other end of town, and even though a lot fewer kids showed up, it all went well. Patrick found the day to be extremely boring. He wasn't allowed to do any huge media stunts or make a spectacular entrance like he usually did, since the producers behind the show found it *inappropriate given the tragedy*.

All that kept Patrick going throughout the day was the prospect of what he had planned for the coming night. The day seemed endless to him when, finally, around three o'clock, he was told the last contestant was up. Patrick wrapped up the last interview with the boy who was going to sing, had him talk about his family and how they struggled financially and how he wanted to help them out by becoming the next Shooting Star.

When he was done, Patrick could finally return to his hotel and get ready. He had found his next victim online. He was actually searching for something else, when he stumbled over her webpage and saw her picture. There was no doubt in his mind. Those eyes he would recognize anywhere.

Patrick checked the web-page once again and looked at her face. Oh, how he was looking forward to this. He giggled and shrieked with joy. Patrick found the butterfly knife in his drawer and then the sewing kit with his strong needle and heavy duty thread, a kit that was intended to be used to sew leather. Patrick hadn't had the time to wash it since he sewed the bowtie onto the girl's skin, so he went into the bathroom and cleaned it now. It had been close with the young girl. A little dangerous and very risky. Patrick didn't mind a little danger; it made it so much more fun and exciting, but this time he had been very close to getting caught. While talking to the woman outside the audition room afterwards, Patrick had realized that he had somehow gotten blood on his fingers, even though he had worn gloves while killing the girl. He had wiped it off on the red cloak, hoping the woman didn't notice, which she didn't. At least, he didn't think she did. Maybe she was just too damn stupid.

They're all so stupid. Freaking morons is what they are. Dumb as rocks.

Patrick laughed and winked at his own reflection. No. No one would ever suspect the host of the most popular TV show in Danish TV history. It was absurd. They all felt like they knew him so well, didn't they? After all, he did come directly into their living rooms week after week. He was almost like family to most of them. The crazy uncle, yes, but still family. And you always believe the best about your family, don't you?

Patrick took off his pants and underwear to take a quick shower. He looked at himself in the mirror naked. He turned his torso in the light. The scars were still there, but only he knew where they were. Plus, the hair growing on his chest was covering them nicely. He lifted his forearm and looked at the scars there as well. They were harder to cover, but it wasn't so important. It made him look tough, he thought.

Patrick dropped his head and looked at his penis. To think that it had once been a part of his forearm was still hard to comprehend. *Forearm phalloplasty* was what they had called it at that hospital in Poland where he'd had it made eight years ago. Patrick still didn't have much sensation in it; they'd told him he had a fifty-one percent chance of being able to have intercourse and erections after the operation. Well, Patrick didn't care much about that anyway. Sex was never on his mind. And certainly not now.

Patrick looked at his hair. He would have to cut it again soon. It was getting long and he hated when it got long. He opened the cabinet and took out some pills and swallowed them. Extra hormones. He'd had to take so many of them the last few years to make the change properly. He needed the male hormone in order to grow chest hair and facial hair like any other man. The eyes, he couldn't change. They still resembled those of a girl, those of Nina, who had once been such a big part of his life.

But now she was gone. He had gotten rid of her right after leaving the rich man's mansion with all the jewelry and all his credit cards that Nina had maxed out to get as much cash out of as possible before she threw them away so she didn't get caught.

At the sex change clinic, they had asked her many questions, but never where her money came from. Three years later, Nina, who was now Patrick, had booked a flight—first class, naturally—and returned to the country he had once been stolen from. An article in the newspaper a couple of months later sent him to audition to become the host of a new TV show.

Patrick got dressed, thinking about how much he loathed that little girl that he had once been. So feeble, so weak, so easy to possess and put in a prison.

"Never again," he mumbled, as he found his hooded sweater and put it on. Before he closed the lid of the computer where his next victim was staring back at him, he read the name of where he was going out loud to himself, making his voice shrill like that of a young girl's.

"Dolls and trinkets. Dolls and trinkets."

49

APRIL 2013

Helle Wickman was feeling good about herself this Sunday afternoon. It had been a busy morning with a lot of tourists wanting to buy small souvenirs to take home before they left the island. The afternoon had been quieter, but Helle liked that, too. Especially since she really didn't need the money. She had plenty and more where that came from. The store was more of a hobby. She had dreamed about opening her own store since childhood.

Helle walked down the row of shelves with dolls and looked at them. Oh, how she adored those beautiful dolls. They had become family to her. And now, with her new boyfriend, it all seemed to be going so well for her, she could hardly believe it. Back when her daughter had gone missing, Helle never thought she was going to feel happy again. To think of all the times she had thought about just ending it, just killing herself and ending all the suffering.

But somehow, she had never done it. It was like she had always known that there was something more for her, that life wasn't finished with her yet. And now she had finally found love. She was being loved by someone else and that made her happy again. Even though she found it hard to love herself.

Helle looked at the picture of her daughter. She had considered removing it from the shop. Putting it away since it always made her sad, it always made her feel bad. Maybe it was about time she started over? Maybe it was time to clean the slate and move on?

Helle sniffled and shook her head. No. No, it wasn't time yet. Maybe later. She turned and walked back to the counter. She sighed and looked out onto the street between shelves that were overly filled with souvenirs. She knew she would have to clean up the window shelves soon, since no one could look inside the store anymore from the outside. But Helle liked it that way. She liked having lots of stuff surrounding her.

A lady stopped and looked at something, then moved on. Helle looked at her watch. It was almost time to close the shop. Maybe she should call it a day already? Get out of here early? She looked onto the street again. No, there were still plenty of tourists out there. The TV show had attracted so many people this weekend, it could easily end up being the best weekend of the year for people with small shops like hers.

Helle decided to go out in the back and grab herself a last cup of coffee. Once she was done with that, she would close up. She was humming in the kitchen when she heard the bell above the door ring, telling her there was someone in the shop.

I knew it. Good thing I didn't close up.

She left the coffee cup on the table in the small kitchen and walked back out, humming and wearing a big smile. She enjoyed entertaining people in her shop. She never knew who would walk through that door and with what background. She liked watching them as they browsed through the store, guessing where they were from and what they were looking for. She always let them look a little on their own before she asked them if she could help with anything. To make them feel comfortable first, let them look at other stuff than what they initially came for, so they might buy something they didn't plan on. Helle loved every little trinket in her store, and she loved how excited people often were when browsing around.

Helle glanced towards the door and noticed it seemed to be a man that had entered. She couldn't quite see his face because of the hood he was wearing. It didn't bother Helle, though. Some people preferred their privacy, and she knew to let him have longer finding what he was looking for than other people. He didn't seem to bring any kids, and that made her feel relaxed. Kids were always the worst. They touched everything and moved it around, and sometimes even broke something then put it back without telling anyone. She had often considered putting up a sign stating *no children* next to the *no dogs allowed* sign, but then again she would probably lose a lot of business. The man's head peeked up behind a row of shelves. Helle smiled.

"Let me know if I can help you with anything," she said.

He didn't answer, so she assumed he was foreigner and tried in German as well. When he still didn't answer, she tried in

English, and finally in Polish, which was the only other language she knew.

The man finally replied, but Helle wasn't sure she liked the answer. At first, she thought she might have translated it wrong, but then he repeated it in Danish.

"Where is your ice cream truck, lady?"

50

APRIL 2013

It was late in the afternoon and I was just lazily hanging out in the living room with my kids when the phone rang. I picked it up.

It was Jack. He was panting, speaking incoherently, stuttering heavily. "Iiiii dddidn't know wwwho else to call. Your dad...your dad needs to cccome. Something...I...I ddon't know how to say this. I've ccalled the pppolice..."

"Easy now, Jack," I interrupted him. I suddenly felt very anxious. What was going on? "Try and calm down. You're not making any sense here. Please, try and tell me from the beginning. What is going on? Where are you?"

I heard him take a couple of deep breaths like he usually did when his stuttering was bad. It helped. "I'm at the shop. Helle's shop. It's bad, Emma."

My heart started beating wildly. I got up from the couch

and walked towards the kitchen. "Helle?" I asked. "Has something happened to Helle?"

Jack was quiet. I could hear he was busy controlling his breath.

"Jack? Please answer me. What happened to her?"

"I was going down to her store to continue my painting. When I opened the back door with my key, I heard a noise from the store. It sounded like an entire shelf of trinkets was being tipped over, and I thought Helle needed help, so I hurried in there. But I was too late. He ran out the front door just as I went in. I didn't see him. Just the door closing. And then I found her..."

"Found her where? How? What happened to her?" I asked, while putting on my jacket.

"She was on the floor. He had stabbed her."

"Is she alive?"

"I checked and she still has a pulse—wait the ambulance is here. I hhhave to go, Emma."

"I'm coming down."

I hung up, then called Maya. "I'm going to town for a couple of hours. Can you look out for your brother?"

My daughter nodded. "Of course. What's going on?"

I leaned over and kissed her cheek, thinking she'd had enough shocks lately, and that she didn't need to know what had happened yet. Not until I knew more at least. "I'll be back later and then I'll explain, alright?"

"You always say that. Can Granddad come over? In case you're going to be really late?"

I sighed and shook my head. "No. Not this time, sweetie.

Granddad has to go with me. I'm going to pick him up on the way."

My daughter shrugged. "Whatever," she said, and turned her back to me.

Thinking I'd have to deal with her later, I rushed out the door. I called my dad from the car and told him he had to come with me, that something bad had happened to Helle. The sound of his voice cracking like it did made me feel so sad. He really loved her.

"How bad is it?" he asked, when I drove up to his house and he jumped inside of the car.

"I don't know, Dad. Jack told me she still had a pulse, but she had been stabbed. The ambulance was just arriving when I talked to him."

When we arrived at the store, the ambulance was still parked outside on the street. Inside the shop, two paramedics were working on Helle, who was now on a stretcher. Blood was all over the floor in a pool. My dad gasped when he saw it. Jack came towards us.

"How is she?" my dad asked.

"She's still alive. They're preparing to take her to the hospital right away. There's a helicopter coming to pick her up outside of town, and she'll be airlifted to the mainland." Up until now, I don't think my dad had realized how serious it was, but he did now. Now that he saw her on the stretcher and saw all the blood.

"Can I go with you?" my dad asked. "I'm her boyfriend. The closest she has to a family."

The paramedics looked at each other, then nodded. My dad kissed me, then ran to catch up with them.

"Me and the kids will take the next ferry and be there as fast as we can," I yelled after him.

Officer Morten was also there and told me not to go too close to the scene of the crime. The forensics team was on their way, he said.

"They haven't left the island, since they're still working at the last crime scene down at the theater. They'll be here soon. They'll have to close the entire area off." He was wearing plastic gloves and putting something in a small bag.

"Is that what I think it is?" I asked.

Officer Morten exhaled. Then he showed me what was in the bag. A small white bowtie, a piece of string, and a needle. "I guess he was interrupted before he could sew it onto her chest."

I felt sick to my stomach as pictures of the girl in the kiosk and the girl in the theater flashed before my eyes.

"But, why Helle?" I asked. "The other victims were much younger. Is he changing preferences?"

Officer Morten shrugged. "Maybe their age doesn't matter."

"Hello?"

The voice came from the back. I walked out there to see who it was. An elderly lady stood in the doorway. "Hi there. Is Helle here?"

I shook my head. "No. No, she's not. She has just been taken to the hospital a minute ago."

The woman looked surprised. "Oh. Oh. Is it serious?"

"I'm afraid so. Who are you?"

"I'm Asta. I just had a new doll that I had made for Helle, and I thought I'd stop by and ask her if she would like to see it, but it can wait till later."

"I'll let her know," I said. The woman left and I went back inside.

"Who was it?" Officer Morten asked.

"Some lady that had a new doll for Helle."

"Asta Kristensen," Officer Morten said.

"That's her."

He tapped on his notepad with his pencil for a few seconds. Then he looked at me. "You know, I never thought about it before, but those two women share more than a passion for dolls with one another."

"Is that so?"

"Yes. Asta also lost her daughter from that playground I was talking about," he said pensively.

I was about to leave when I suddenly stopped. "She did?"

"Come to think of it, I believe Asta's daughter was the first one to go missing. It was back in '97. The story is that she went a little nuts after losing her daughter. She was admitted several times to an institution on the mainland before she finally found the passion for dolls to keep her sane. She works as a taxidermist, you know, stuffs animals for museums and people who want them in their houses. The dolls are just her hobby and she sells them to Helle for extra profit, as far as I know. It's a little sad, her story, that is. We used to call her Miss Polly. Because of the song, you know. And all her dolls. She has the house filled with them and she treats them like real children. She dresses them every day and puts them in a stroller and takes them for a walk. Some people say she even feeds them and talks to them all day. Guess it's a little sad."

51

APRIL 2013

The woman was often gone for hours at a time. Josephine was left in the darkness only accompanied by Django, who was put in the room with her to make sure she didn't try and escape.

Josephine no longer knew how long she had spent in the cage in the woman's basement. And she was getting too tired to think about it anymore. All she wanted to do was to sleep. The woman had hardly given her any food, only a few crackers now and then that she fed her through the bars. Josephine could feel that she was losing weight. Her arms had become very thin and the skin on her stomach was drooping. Every day, the woman would come down to the basement and feel the skin on Josephine's arm. It reminded Josephine of the story of Hansel and Gretel, only it didn't seem like she wanted Josephine to get fatter.

Josephine didn't understand it at all. If the woman wanted to eat Josephine, wouldn't she want her to be fat? Why didn't she feed her then? It made no sense.

Josephine was too tired to even try and plead with her anymore. The first days she had begged and pleaded for her to give her more food, but the woman had pretended not to hear. She was good at that. Only Django seemed to listen when Josephine spoke.

Josephine sighed in the darkness. She tried to move to change position, but her body was aching all over. It was truly painful. She was so tired of being in this cage, so tired of being afraid of what was going to happen to her, so tired of lying awake all night listening to her stomach growl, feeling the pain of hunger.

Django lifted his head and looked at her. Since she had gotten skinnier Josephine was now able to put her arm out through the bars and reach Django. She petted him on his head. He seemed to like that. They had become quite good friends lately, and as long as Josephine stayed put, he was very nice to her. As soon as she tried to shake the bars or scream or fiddle with the lock, he would start growling and snapping his teeth at her. If she behaved, he was really nice. And since he was her only companion in this godforsaken basement, Josephine tried to be good. She succeeded most of the time.

Josephine heard a rattle behind the door and knew the woman was unlocking it from the outside. She drew back her arm and looked at the door opening with anxious eyes. The woman entered. She was humming, as usual.

Django got up on his feet and ran towards her while wagging his tail. "Hi there, buddy. How are we doing today? Is she behaving?" she asked, patting his back.

Django made a satisfied grunt. The woman pulled out a treat from her pocket and gave it to him. Josephine listened to the crunching sound coming from his mouth as he ate the treat and wished so badly that she could get one, too.

Mommy, I'm so hungry. Please, come find me. Please, help me.

Josephine knew her parents had to be searching for her, and for days she had thought about finding a way to communicate with the outside world, but without any luck. She wished so badly to be able to tell the world where she was, to scream to people walking by on the street outside of the house. But she had already tried. Screaming didn't get her anywhere. It only made her unpopular with the old woman and Django.

The woman approached Josephine's cage and looked at her like she was examining her.

"Give me your arm," she said.

Josephine obeyed and stuck out her arm between the bars. The old woman felt it and pulled the skin. "Yes, yes. I think you're right. It's looking good now, Django. I think she is ready for the next step."

Josephine gasped as the woman pulled her loose skin hard again. Then she smiled. "We're gonna peel all that skin off of you like you were a chicken, aren't we Django? Yes, we are. All of this nice loose skin will come right off once we get started, just you wait and see. And then we're gonna stuff you like a bird. Yes. I think we are. To make you last forever and ever. To make you stay beautiful forever. Isn't that wonderful...*baby doll?*"

52

APRIL 2013

We spent all day and most of the evening at the hospital in Esbjerg, the town on the mainland closest to the island. Helle was stable they told us, but not awake yet, and they weren't expecting her to wake up any time before tomorrow, but it might also take longer than that. Maybe even several days. She had lost a lot of blood and they couldn't tell us yet if there had been any damage to her brain.

Later, they told us to go home and get a good night's rest. There wasn't really much for us to do but wait, and we might as well do that at home. So, we did. We took the ferry back to the island and made it home before midnight. Maya and Victor were exhausted, so I got them to bed right away. My dad was sitting in the kitchen when I came back down.

"Can I get you anything?" I asked.

He was sitting with his head bowed. Now he looked at me. I hated to see him like this.

"What do you say we grab a beer?" I asked.

He nodded heavily. I opened the refrigerator and pulled out two beers. We drank in silence for a little while. I put my hand on top of his. He sipped his beer and swallowed. Then he looked at me.

"I just don't understand why," he said. "You say this killer has many victims on his conscience, but why of all the people in the world would he pick Helle?"

I shrugged. "Why would he pick the young girl at the auditions? I think we all want an explanation, but maybe there isn't one. Maybe he just picks his victims randomly, victims of opportunity."

My dad sniffled and drank again. "Maybe you're right."

"Can you think of any reason why anyone would have anything against Helle?" I asked.

"Nah. You're right. She's just a nice lady with a funny shop. Why would anyone want to harm her?"

My dad finished his beer, then looked at me. "That hit the spot. Do you mind me crashing here?"

"I was expecting you to. Take any room upstairs."

He growled and got up. "I would have sworn I'd never have to sleep in this awful house again, but I really don't want to be alone tonight, you know?"

I smiled. "I know, Dad. You're always welcome here."

My dad grunted and left the room. I still had way too much adrenalin in my blood to be able to sleep, so I pulled a second beer from the refrigerator. I went into the living room and grabbed my computer. I started researching the bowtie killer. Using what my ex-boyfriend once taught me, I hacked into the

Danish police force's central database and found all the files and cases and went through them one after the other. He had killed many over the years, but mostly younger women and teenage girls. Not one of them had been older like Helle. It surprised me, but then again it could just be a coincidence. I scrolled through the notes the two officers working on the case had written and then stopped. A particular sentence stuck out to me. One of the theories the police were working with was that the killer was some kind of *stalker of the TV show "Shooting Stars."* They based the theory on the fact that most of the killings happened on the last night the TV show was in town or right after they had left town. That caused the police conclude that someone was following the TV show around killing people in its tail.

I looked up and drank some more of my beer. *Hadn't anyone thought about the fact that it might be someone connected to the TV show instead?* I thought to myself. There were hundreds of people working on a show like this. One of them could easily be a psychopath. Sick people were everywhere, and often a guy like this, a true psychopath, was brilliant at hiding, at blending into a crowd. At least that was what I had read.

I returned to my computer and tried a new approach. I knew my dad was going to hate me for this, but I did it anyway. I hacked my way into Helle's computer in her shop and started going through her stuff. A lot of it was personal, and I promised myself to never tell my dad about anything I encountered in there.

I checked her emails to see if anyone had contacted her in the last couple of days, maybe someone from the TV show, but found nothing. I moved on to check her Internet browsing history the last few days. She had been visiting a lot of pages about dolls, then Facebook, some news websites, where she mostly read stuff about royalty and celebrities. Then there were literally hundreds of pages where she had read about the disappearance of Josephine Gyldenstjerne, *the lost Countess*, as they had named her. It wasn't so strange that she would be interested in that case, since she naturally saw many similarities with her own story. I sighed and leaned back into the couch. I pulled the laptop onto my chest and found a way into Helle's web-bank by guessing her password, which happened to be *dollbaby*. I drank the rest of my beer and almost dropped it when the page opened up and I saw how much money she had in her account.

I stared at it for a long time to make sure I wasn't mistaken. Then, I closed the lid of the computer and took it with me up the stairs. As I turned off the light and lay under the covers, I knew I was going to have to break my promise to myself.

53

APRIL 2013

I had printed everything out for my dad to see when he got down the next morning. I knew it would be a little much for him after what he had been through the day before, but I had to show him. I couldn't know this and not tell him. Why she had chosen to keep it a secret from my dad was her business; she probably had her reasons, but there was no way I could keep this from him. The damage was done.

I was still bent over the stove making scrambled eggs when I heard a grunt behind my back. I turned and smiled.

"Good morning, Dad."

"Humph. Where are the kids?"

"They've left for school. It's Monday."

I poured him some coffee and placed it in front of him. He grunted something that was probably supposed to be a *thank you*. My dad had never been a morning person, and today less than ever.

"Any news about Helle?" I asked.

He shook his head. "They promised they would call if she woke up. I slept with the damn phone next to my head all night. Now I have the worst headache. I'm not so sure these things are healthy for you."

"Here, have some orange juice," I said, and poured him a glass. "I'm also making eggs."

My dad shook his head and growled. He drank the juice. "I'm not hungry, but thanks. I'd like to get to the hospital as soon as possible. I want to be there when she wakes up. They said it was going to be today."

"Dad, they said it *might* be today. There is a difference."

He grunted, dissatisfied. "Whatever."

I put the papers on the table in front of him.

"What's this?" he said.

I sat down with my coffee cup in my hand. "Look, Dad. I know you're going through a lot of stuff right now, but I did some research last night, and I think there are some things you need to know about Helle."

He looked startled. "Like what?"

I took out a piece of paper and pointed at the number on top showing the total amount of money in her account. My dad whistled, impressed. He took it from my hand and looked again. "That's a lot of money."

"It's Helle's bank account."

My dad laughed. "No. It can't be. You must be mistaken."

"I hacked into her bank account last night, and this is what I found."

"You hacked into her bank account? Why on earth would you do such an awful thing?"

"I was checking out her personal stuff to make sure she hadn't spoken to someone or chatted with someone that might be the killer."

"But still. Emma. She is my girlfriend. You're not allowed to do something like that. It's private. Besides, why her bank account? I can understand her email and things like that, but her bank?"

I blushed. He was right. I had no explanation. I had been curious, that was all, but it was no excuse. I felt bad and tried not to show it. "It doesn't matter. The fact is, I did it, and I can't help wondering where she got all those millions from. Haven't you ever wondered where she gets her money from? I mean, it's definitely not the small shop downtown. If anything, she's only losing money on that."

He shrugged. "Maybe she inherited the money, maybe she won the lottery, or maybe she got it in the divorce from her ex. Who knows?"

"Maybe. Was he rich?"

"Not that I know of." My dad sipped his coffee. "I'm sure there is a perfectly good explanation for all of this," my dad said, and got up from the chair.

"I'm sure there is. And it's none of my business, I know that."

I put my coffee cup in the sink and looked at my dad. He suddenly seemed so old. Maybe it was just the sadness in his eyes. I was overwhelmed with guilt. Should I have kept quiet about this, after all? No, done was done. My dad needed to know this. He deserved to know, and even if it turned out to be nothing at all, I still wanted him to know. After all, it was going to come out anyway once the police started investigating her to see if there was any motive for attacking her. This was a good motive. Money was always a good motive.

"Do you want me to take you to the hospital to see her today?" I asked.

My dad nodded. "That would be nice, thanks."

54

———————

APRIL 2013

I t had gone wrong, terribly wrong. Patrick felt like a failure when he drove towards the port where tonight's big show was going to take place. They were building the stage now and Patrick was supposed to have been at the noon briefing several minutes ago.

But, somehow, he just wasn't quite in the mood for it. Not for any of it. It wasn't like a catastrophe, he had managed to hurt the red-haired woman like he wanted to, and she had even looked at him and known at that instant that it was revenge, that it was her past coming back to haunt her. But he hadn't managed to kill her or leave his mark, his brand, behind. Someone had interrupted him and he'd had to run.

"Damn it," he mumbled, and hit his fist on the leather seat.

Hanne, sitting next to him in the island's only limousine, which they had rented for the day, looked at him. "What's up with you today?" she asked.

Patrick pulled out one of his famous smiles. "Nothing. Just excited about the show," he said emotionlessly.

Patrick had heard about the woman on the radio in the morning while he was in the shower. They had said that a woman was found yesterday in her own shop where someone had attempted to murder her, but apparently the killer was interrupted and ran off.

Attempted?

Yes, that meant she was still alive in the hospital on the mainland. Yes, that meant the doctors believed she was going to survive, the speaker said.

"It's the first time a victim has survived an encounter with the bowtie killer," were the last words Patrick heard before he threw the radio against the mirror and broke both.

Survived? She was still alive?

Patrick clenched his fist and fantasized about knocking Hanne out while in the car. He restrained himself. At least the woman wasn't awake yet and couldn't speak. The speaker on the radio had said so. She was still unconscious. That meant she couldn't spill the beans on Patrick just yet. That meant he still had time to finish his project, to finish what he'd come back for. That, at least, was something. Patrick burst into laughter thinking about what he had planned for later today, this afternoon before the big show. They always gave him a couple of hours to rest and get himself all psyched up for the big show. Oh, he was going to get psyched up alright. No doubt about that.

Patrick laughed again. Hanne stared at him again. He smiled crazily. She looked confused. Then she shook her head.

"You sure are something, Patrick." The limo entered the area in front of the stage next to the port. Screaming fans approached the windows and started knocking, while pressing their breasts against the car.

"Patrick, Patrick, Patrick."

Hanne scoffed. "I still don't get it. Maybe I never will. But they do love you. So do the producers. But only as long as you bring home the ratings, you understand that? One bad move that makes people switch the channel or turn off the TV, and you're out of here. That's the way it works, okay, baby doll?"

Patrick turned his head and looked at her. For years, he had looked for a good reason to kill Hanne other than her being a complete pain in the neck. He had been going back and forth on the subject, not knowing if he wanted to or not, waiting for the perfect time, the perfect excuse.

And here she was handing it to him on a silver platter.

"Why are you looking at me like that, Patrick?" she asked and pulled away from him.

He laughed manically. Then he leaned over and pressed his lips against hers. She protested heavily, but Patrick grabbed her around the neck and started to squeeze it, holding her down with the weight of his body so she couldn't move. He forced his tongue into her mouth while she fought to get him off. As soon as he let go of her lips, she started screaming, but his grip on her throat was too tight for much other than spurting sounds to emerge. Patrick smiled and stroked her gently across her face before he knocked her out with a head-butt. After that, she didn't fight much as he strangled her, once again feeling the almighty thrill of power and control. He panted and leaned back in the leather seat, finally feeling like his good old self again.

The driver forced the limo through the crowd of screaming fans and drove to the back of the stage, where Patrick took Hanne in his arms and carried her into his dressing room, telling people on the way how she had fallen asleep in the car.

"I think she drank a little heavily last night, if you ask me," he said, and laughed to one of the security guys guarding the door to his room.

Much to his surprise, the guy laughed back.

55

APRIL 2013

W hen we arrived at the hospital, it was packed with police cars outside the front entrance. We walked in, but were stopped in the main hall by a man in uniform.

"Listen. My girlfriend is in there down that hall..." my dad started.

"I'm sorry," the police officer said. "I have been told to let no one through."

"You can let these two come in," a voice behind him said. It was Officer Morten. I smiled when I saw him. "They're okay," he said to the officer, who backed down and stepped out of the way.

"What's with all the police?" my dad said, as Officer Morten showed us down the hallway towards Helle's room.

"Protection, in case the killer tries to finish Helle off. She is, after all, the first to have ever survived an encounter with the bowtie killer. He has reason to want to keep her quiet. Plus, she is awake now, so we're questioning her to get more details about the killer."

"She's awake?" my dad almost yelled.

"Yes," Officer Morten said with a big smile, until he noticed my dad's angry red face.

"Why haven't they called me? I was told they would call me first thing when she woke up!" he said.

"She has just woken up, like half an hour ago, I think. I'm pretty sure the investigators wanted to have her a little to themselves, too. You know, to get all the information they need to catch the killer."

"Have they gotten anything yet?" I asked, when we stopped outside a door. Four police officers were guarding it. We heard voices from inside the room.

"Not as far as I know. But they haven't been in there for long. The doctor had to check that she was up for it first."

We waited at least twenty minutes outside her room before an officer finally came out. Officer Morten looked at him expectantly. He shrugged and shook his head. "She won't talk," he said.

"Won't she say anything?" I asked.

The officer looked at me questioningly.

"They're family," Officer Morten said. "This is Officer Nyberg, he's on the case investigating the bowtie killer," he said to us.

"All she says is she can't remember anything. She can't remember who attacked her or even how," Officer Nyberg said with a tired sigh.

Officer Morten nodded. "Well, it's not unusual after being unconscious for this long, I guess."

"No, it's not. But I have a feeling that she's lying. She does remember, but she's scared or something. It's just a hunch, but a pretty strong one."

Officer Morten nodded.

"Why don't you let us talk to her?" I asked.

Both policemen stared at me.

"My dad is dating her, and I've gotten quite close to her lately, as well. Maybe she'll talk to us?"

Officer Morten shrugged and looked at the other guy. "Guess it's at least worth a try."

Officer Nyberg looked at me. "This might not be such a bad idea. Are you up for it? It might be ugly. I mean, if she starts talking, she might tell you details that can be tough to handle. Can you deal with that? All you have to do is to get her to open up to you. We'll take over as soon as possible. All we need is for her to describe the damn killer for us, so we can nail the bastard. Just make her talk, could you do that?"

I looked at my dad. "We can do this," I said and grabbed his hand. "Right, Dad?"

56

APRIL 2013

"I already told the police I don't remember anything. Nothing at all," Helle said. She looked horrible. Pale and in obvious pain when she tried to talk.

"Just tell us what you do remember," my dad said. "We need to help them catch the guy. I want to put him away for a long time." My dad held Helle's hand in his. I could hear anger in his voice. "We need to help them stop him before he does this to someone else."

"Didn't you see anything?" I asked. "Maybe his hair or eyes?"

Helle turned her face away. "I told you I don't remember anything about him. All I remember is pouring myself some coffee while he entered the store, then walking out there and asking him if he needed any help. Then it all went black after that."

"Didn't you catch a glimpse of him before it went black?" I asked.

"I couldn't see properly. It was dark, he was standing behind the shelves wearing a hood over his head. You know, one of those sweaters with a hood on. I remember the sweater was dark blue, that's all. I already told this to the police."

"Did it say anything on his sweater?" I asked.

She shook her head. I could tell it hurt.

"Maybe we should stop," my dad said. "She needs her rest."

I exhaled and nodded. "I think you're right."

"I mean there was something about him that felt awfully familiar," Helle said, all of a sudden.

"Yes? Like what?" my dad asked.

She shook her head again. It hurt and she closed her eyes to the pain. "I don't know...maybe it was his eyes, maybe I did catch a glimpse of them after all. I remember thinking I knew them from somewhere, but I couldn't quite understand where from. Then there was his voice. I think I heard it somewhere before. I don't know. It's all very blurry."

"Can you think of any reason why anyone would attack you like that?" I asked.

"No," she answered promptly. "The police asked the same question."

"Maybe it was your money," my dad blurted out. He looked at me like he regretted that he said it.

Helle turned her head and looked directly at him. "That was also what the police said," she answered.

I sighed, relieved. If the police already asked her this, it wasn't strange that we did as well.

"They also asked me where I had gotten all that money from," she continued.

"What did you tell them?" my dad asked.

She looked at my dad, then pulled her hand out of his. "You know what? I don't owe you two anything. I don't have to explain myself to you. You come here and ask me all these questions like I am some kind of criminal here, but I'm not, alright? I'm not the criminal. I'm the victim. I was the one who was attacked. I'm in pain here, and I'd really appreciate it if you two would just leave."

My dad looked perplexed. "But, Helle. We're just trying to help out here. The police wanted us to try and see if we could help you remember more."

"The police?" Helle almost yelled, but it was too painful. She completely lost the little bit of color she had regained in her face. "You work for the police now, questioning me? How could you do this to me?"

"But, we're just trying to help," my dad said.

"Well, you're not helping me. Who says I want your help anyway? Who says I even want you here?"

"But...But, Helle?"

"You know what? I'm sick of you. Sick and tired of you and your ridiculous family snooping around in my business. Sick of your daughter's problems that always have to become your problems, too; I don't care about her and all her crap. I don't understand why I have to be dragged into all your problems again and again. She's a grown woman, for Christ sake. Let her handle her stuff on her own. It's sick that she still needs her daddy to help her out constantly and do everything for her. You people make me sick."

"Helle, my dad's only trying..."

Before I could finish the sentence, she hissed at the both of us,

"Get out. Get out of here now. Get out of my life."

APRIL 2013

My dad was very quiet in the car on the way home. I felt really sad for him. Once on the ferry, we walked onto the top deck to get some fresh air.

My dad leaned on the railing and looked at the island approaching in the distance. He shook his head heavily. "I just don't understand. Do you, Emma?"

"I...I really don't, Dad."

"What got into her? She used to be so sweet. She never raised her voice like that before. Nor did she ever complain about my family. Why would she say those things, Emma?"

I shrugged and looked down at the water beneath the ferry. The cold wind was biting my cheeks. "I wish I could explain that to you, but I really can't. I don't know her very well, but to be fair she did just suffer a serious trauma. Maybe if you gave her a little time?"

My dad shook his head. "No. I can't. Not after what she

said. My family is everything to me. You, the kids, you're all I have, and I'd do anything for you. I can't be with a woman who doesn't understand that. I just can't."

"Maybe she'll apologize later on," I said. "Maybe it was the medicine talking, or something else. The stress of being interrogated by the police? I don't know."

My dad shook his head again. "It was strange seeing her like that. Did you look into her eyes? It was like they were suddenly filled with hatred. I felt like she suddenly really hated me. It came right after I asked about the money. Now I can't stop wondering why she doesn't want to talk about the money."

We went back to the car as the ferry approached land. When we drove across the parking lot, my dad looked at the big stage they had put up at the port.

"The show is tonight," I said. "I completely forgot about that. I promised Maya she could go see it. Ida is going to sing on stage. We should all be there and cheer on her."

My dad chuckled. "What do you think Victor is going to say about that?"

"Oh no. Victor," I said. "I'm never going to persuade him to come down here. He'll hate all the people and the noise. Maybe I should just stay home then."

My dad put his hand on my shoulder. "No, you go. I'll stay at your house with Victor."

"Would you really do that?"

"Sure. Him and me are buddies, remember? It'll do us some good to hang out a little. Both of us, I think. I need some quiet time, and so does he. It'll be good; don't you worry."

"Thanks, Dad. I appreciate it. I know Sophia will be so

happy that I can go. Her mother has come down here to take care of the other kids while she goes to watch Ida in the show. She's been looking forward to this. And, frankly, so have I. I can't wait to see little Ida up on the stage. She surprised everyone with her big voice at the auditions. I had no idea she had it in her. She's usually so shy."

"It's always the quiet ones that surprise us the most," my dad said with a little smile.

It felt good to see him smile again. Even though it was still with sadness in his eyes. I hated to see him heartbroken like this. He really didn't deserve it. I drove the car into the driveway and parked it in front of my grandmother's old house. I looked at the clock in the kitchen when we entered. Victor and Maya would be home from school any minute now. Perfect timing. My dad walked into the living room and sat in an armchair. I approached him.

"Do you want some coffee or anything else?"

"No thanks, I'm good," he said.

It startled me slightly. He never said no to a cup of coffee. "Can I get the paper for you?" I asked.

He shook his head. "Maybe a little later."

"Oh, okay." I walked to the kitchen and started making a pot of coffee. My stomach had turned to knots. I felt so angry with Helle for treating him like this. As the coffee ran through the coffeemaker, I started feeling guilty for having brought up the subject of the money at all. Would she have reacted so angrily if my dad had never known about the money?

I shook my head and poured myself a cup. No, there was definitely something wrong with this woman, and I concluded that I should only be glad that my dad discovered it now and not later when he had become even more emotionally involved. This was a good thing, even though it didn't feel like it was.

I decided to pour him a cup of coffee anyway, and placed it on the end table next to his chair. He was staring out the window at the big trees in the back yard that I so desperately wanted to cut down so we could see the ocean from the house, but couldn't, since it would kill Victor. It was his playground and the only place in this world he actually liked to be. I had to live without the view.

He didn't notice the coffee. He seemed deep into his own thoughts, so I decided to let him be and grabbed my laptop. I sat on the couch and started going through my research. I hadn't gotten much more information for my book and it annoyed me slightly. I really wanted to write the book about the children being kidnapped from the island.

I opened an article about the first disappearance in 1997. Nina Kristensen, six years old. Once again, I looked at the picture of the girl and the doll that had been found on the ground. I sipped my coffee. I found another article about the same case. This time it was an interview with the mother, who was pleading for people on the island to please help her find her precious daughter. I felt a pinch in my heart, thinking about my own children and trying to imagine what it must feel like to lose your child like that. It made me almost sick with sadness. Then I thought about Helle and how losing her daughter must have been devastating for her, and maybe, maybe that was part of the explanation why she seemed so troubled, why she seemed almost like she had a split personality. She definitely had a side to her that was quite scary, and maybe it was for the better that my dad stopped seeing her now before she showed more of her hidden side. Even if it did mean he was back to grumbling and moping again.

I looked down at the article again and at the picture of the mother in the interview. I remembered seeing her in Helle's store and that Officer Morten had told me how they each shared the same tragic story. I wondered if they both knew? If they ever talked to each other about it?

I read the name underneath her picture. Asta Kristensen. Then I searched for her name in the yellow pages and found her address. It wasn't far away from the playground that Officer Morten had told me all the girls had disappeared from. I had long wanted to go see that playground. Maybe I should pay Mrs. Kristensen a visit while down there? Talk to her about the book and ask her if she would be interested in doing an interview for it? I needed as many of the mothers as possible to be able to even write the book in the first place. If they all turned me down, I would have to give it up anyway, so I figured I might as well begin there. Face to face was the best way to address this. If I just called her, it would be too easy for her to decline my request.

I wrote the address down on a small piece of paper, then got up from the couch. "I have to run some errands, Dad. The kids will be back from school any minute now."

"I'm not going anywhere. Go do your thing," he answered.

"Okay, Dad. Thanks. It's a big help. I'll get back and fix you dinner. The concert starts at six."

"I've got this, sweetheart."

"I don't like to leave you when you feel like this, Dad. Are you sure it's okay?" I asked with a sigh.

"I'm fine, Emma. Really. The kids will cheer me up. Being with them always makes me feel good. Don't worry. You know I hate it when you worry about me. I'm a grown man. I can handle a broken heart."

I leaned over and kissed his forehead. He patted me on the shoulder, and then I left.

58

APRIL 2013

After the briefing, Patrick slipped into a disguise and managed to find a cab to drive him to the other end of town. It had been sixteen years since he was last in this neighborhood, but he remembered every little detail about it; every corner, every house, every streetlamp brought back memories of the childhood he had spent here before his mother gave him away. Before she cast him into a world of abuse, uncertainty, and constant fear for his life. He had come to terms with it over the years and realized she probably did it to toughen him up, to teach him the way of life...that nothing came easily, and so on. Yes, he had many explanations for why his mother had given him away to those people who had abused him over and over again. But he was never able to forgive her. And now it was time to settle the score; it was time for her to face her past and what she had done.

Patrick giggled, thinking about how great it was going to be as he walked onto the street of his childhood home and passed the playground. Then he stopped for just a short second and looked at all the children playing without a care in the world. It always annoyed him to see children happy. It reminded him of the fact that he had never been like them, that he never had the chance to just play without a care in the world. Not even when he lived with his mother. She would always dress him up in these horrible dresses and tell him not to get dirty or even play with other kids. One good thing she had taught him, though, was that he was special, that he was different and that one day he was going to make the world love him and run after him. And she had been right. He was the single most popular TV host in the country right now. If you went into a store, his face was on the covers of all the magazines. They either loved him or they loved to hate him. Patrick couldn't help chuckling, thinking that maybe his mother didn't quite picture it being in this way. But he had done it in his own way, hadn't he? Yes, he had. Like in that famous old song, he had done it *my way*. And for that, he was proud. He wasn't just another pretty face.

Looking at the children, remembering how much he hated wearing those dresses, he realized it had started way back then. He had always felt like he was trapped in the wrong body. It wasn't just that he had come to hate everything about himself being a girl, who was so weak that she was constantly abused. It had always been like that. And his mother hadn't wanted to listen. She had refused to let him wear pants like he'd wanted to. Instead, she had put ugly bowties in his hair and on his dresses. How he loathed her for that. She was the reason for everything bad happening in his life.

Patrick took one last glimpse at the children playing, laughing, and yelling happily. A girl was on the swings singing a song. Part of him wanted to grab her and slit her throat, just to make her shut up.

There is nothing to be so cheerful about, little baby doll. The world is a cruel place, and soon you'll see it, too. Then you'll never want to sing again. I make that promise to you.

Patrick smiled manically, fantasizing about killing the girl, and how the happiness in her eyes would disappear and never return. How he would shut that door of hope in her heart once she realized no one would ever be able to save her from this, how not even her precious mommy or daddy were going to be able to help her.

But this is not the time, he thought, and let go of the fantasy. He took a deep breath and remembered the smells of his childhood. Then, he walked on. In the distance, he spotted the grey house. His heart started racing and his steps became slower. He remembered the door, the windows that he used to stare out of, dreaming about the world on the outside that he would one day conquer. Dreaming about escaping the house that he had back then seen as a prison, escaping his mother's long claws that held him back, held him so tight to herself, wondering if she would ever let go of him enough so he could go out and fulfill his purpose? Reach his dreams?

Patrick approached the house with slow steps, taking deep breaths to calm his rapidly beating heart. He was overwhelmed with a sadness that soon turned into more anger. He peeked in through the window. There she was. Right there, inside the living room, he spotted her. But she wasn't alone. Patrick cursed. There was a woman there with her. His mother was serving her coffee and they were talking. He mumbled and cursed again while staring at them through the window.

Then he smiled. *You'll just have to kill the both of them, now won't you?*

59

———————

APRIL 2013

The dolls everywhere creeped me out. I was sitting in Asta Kristensen's living room and felt like the entire room was staring at me. Hundreds of sets of eyes looking at me without blinking. It was about to freak me out. Especially since the woman insisted on talking to the dolls constantly like they were alive, like they were her children.

I sipped the coffee and wondered if I would even be able to get a decent interview out of her for the book. Was she even sane enough?

I smiled when she offered me a home baked cookie. I took one and ate it while Asta offered all of her dolls one as well. I had to try really hard to hold back my laughter. It was so comical and weird. I bit my lip. Apparently, the doll constantly on Asta's lap wanted one, and it was held against her mouth while Asta made eating sounds with her mouth, then ended up eating it for the doll.

"Was that good, Little Miss Jasmine?" she asked. The doll nodded. "Want one more?" It nodded again. "Now, not too many or you'll get a tummy ache, Little Miss Jasmine. And we can't have that, now can we?"

The doll shook its head. I recognized it from the pictures in the papers. It was the same doll that had been found after the girl disappeared. The one without hair. The one that looked like a baby. I felt a little uncomfortable, kind of like I had crashed a private party. The woman hardly spoke to me or even looked at me. I grabbed another cookie from the plate.

"No. No more for you, Little Miss Jasmine. You've had your share," she said to the doll.

I cleared my throat, trying to get her attention. I succeeded. She finally looked at me. "So, tell me, Miss Emma Frost. What can I do for you?"

"Well, as I said when I knocked on the door, I'm a writer and I'm writing a book about the children that have gone missing over the years from the island. And I was wonde—"

"Just one second," she interrupted me and turned to face the two dolls behind her. "Now, stop fighting, Anna and Lotte. Don't make me come back there. Mommy's busy talking to the nice lady now. So, you have to be quiet, okay?"

The dolls stared at her with their empty eyes. "Good," Asta said, and raised her finger at them. "Now, behave."

She turned to look at me again. "Sorry about that. Where were we?"

"I was just saying that I am trying to write my book, and I would love to feature the mothers of the children in it as well. And I was wondering if you would like to be a part of it. I would have to do a longer interview with you about the life you had before with your daughter in the house and details about the day she disappeared, and of course what happened in the days afterwards, the police investigation, the search, and all that happened, and then about how you are doing today. What your life is like and how often you think about your daughter, if you believe she could still be alive, and so on." I sipped my coffee, noticing how Asta was suddenly staring at me.

"But Nina drowned," she said. "Why would I think she was still alive when she drowned in the ocean?"

I swallowed hard and bit my tongue. I had said too much. After all, nothing was concluded yet, it was all just theories based on what Officer Morten and I had figured out. It was way too early to say anything to the families yet. Way too early.

Me and my big mouth.

I shook my head trying to save it. "No. No. Of course not. But the thing is the body was never found, so maybe you were still wondering if she could be alive. I could imagine that...as a mom myself I would be wondering...until you had closure, you know."

She looked confused. "I'm not sure—?" She looked down at the doll in her hand. "What did you say, Little Miss Jasmine? You're getting tired. Yes, Mommy's tired, too. Having guests is exhausting, isn't it?"

"I...I didn't mean to..." I stopped myself. This wasn't going well. I got up from the couch. I was about to say something when a distant scream interrupted me. It wasn't just an ordinary scream, like children playing.

It was a scream for help.

APRIL 2013

Josephine had heard voices coming from upstairs. For the first time since she had been locked inside the cage, she heard voices other than the old woman's, and she had started screaming.

Josephine didn't have much strength left after being starved for so long, but hearing the voices and footsteps so close caused her heart rate to go up and the adrenalin to rush through her body, renewing her strength, giving her the power to scream at the top of her lungs once again, while hammering her fists into the bars of her cage.

Django immediately rose to his feet and started barking at her, and together, they were making a lot of noise.

"Heeeeeeeelp!" she screamed. "I'm down here. I'm in a cage. Please help me. Please HELP!"

Josephine felt so tired, she put her face on the bars while catching her breath. She looked at the door leading upstairs with anticipation, with the last small bit of hope she could gather. Oh, how many times she had fantasied about being rescued, about someone other than the old lady coming through that door. And how many times she had been so deeply disappointed. Hope was all she had, and she was about to run out of that, too.

There it was again. She heard the muffled voices again. This time, she could hear what they said. They had to be close to the door now.

"What was that?" someone asked.

"I didn't hear anything," the old woman said.

"It sounded like someone screaming."

"Probably just the neighbor's kids playing."

"No, someone was crying for help. It sounded like it came from inside this house," the strange voice said.

Josephine was breathing heavily, trying hard to gather enough strength to scream again. She looked at Django, who had stopped barking, and was now watching her while snapping his teeth at her. Josephine clung on to the small glimpse of that precious hope that she had actually managed to draw a stranger's attention and let her know she was down there.

"I'm sure it was just the neighbors," the old woman said. "Those kids are always playing around in the yard."

"Well, maybe you're right. It did sound like it was far away."

No. No. Don't give up. I'm down here, don't go. Please don't leave, Josephine thought. She took in a deep breath and tried hard to open her mouth and scream again. But only a small shriek left her mouth. It made Django bark again.

"Do you have a dog?" the strange voice said in the distance.

It seemed so far away now. Like in a completely different universe, Josephine thought, as she closed her eyes and slowly started dozing off.

No. No. You have to stay awake, Josephine. Don't drift away or the lady will be gone and never come back. Not now.

"No. That has to be the neighbors also," the old woman said.

The voices seemed so far away now. It was like they didn't matter anymore to Josephine. It was like nothing mattered anymore.

"Ah, okay. I see. The neighbors have lots of screaming children and a noisy dog. Must be very annoying."

"I live with it," the old woman said.

Come on, Josephine. You can do it. Just open your mouth and do it. Just scream. Let out any sound to let her know you're down here. It's not that hard. Just open your mouth and scream. Scream, for crying out loud.

Josephine felt her dry and cracked lips part and she took in a breath. As pictures of her mother and father and the wide sandy beach flickered before her eyes, she finally let out a sound. A small and still, *help me, please help me*, left her lips. In her mind, it sounded like she was screaming, but to the surrounding world, it sounded like nothing more than her last dying breath.

61

———

APRIL 2013

It was all very strange, I thought, and looked at Asta standing in front of me. The screams, the dog barking. I couldn't put my finger on it, but something didn't seem right. It wasn't just all the dolls and the talking to them as if they were real. It was everything about this woman.

Maybe I was just being paranoid. Seeing my dad's girlfriend change her attitude like that had maybe made me slightly suspicious.

Yes, that was it.

"I better leave now," I said.

"Do come again another time," Asta chirped. "Little Miss Jasmine really likes you."

I looked at Asta, then turned to walk towards the front door, when suddenly I spotted a bowl of dog food on the kitchen floor. And one for water right next to it. I turned on my heel to look at Asta.

"No dog, huh?"

"I can explain...it's for...my dolls."

"Yeah, right," I said, and stormed past her. It was about time I followed my instincts. There was something really wrong here. I thought of Victor's strange behavior in the middle of the night, I thought about the bowties that all the dolls were wearing. I couldn't put the pieces together just yet, but I knew somehow that I was close.

I approached the door that I thought I heard the screaming coming from. A dog was definitely barking behind it now. I tried to open it, but it was locked.

"Open it, please," I said.

Asta shook her head. "You have no right. I want you out of my house right now. This is not ri—"

I didn't wait for her to finish the sentence. Instead I backed up, lifted my leg, and kicked down the door. The old door splintered completely. Asta yelled at me, but I didn't care. I walked down the stairs. I stopped as I reached the bottom. The stench made me sick to my stomach. A dog was looking at me. Behind it, I saw something that made my heart stop. A little girl in a cage. I didn't recognize her at first, since she had lost a lot of weight, but as soon as I approached her, I had no doubt in my mind that it was the Countess that had gone missing.

"What the hell is going on here?" I yelled.

The dog growled at me, but I picked up a stick and swung it to scare it off. That helped. The dog backed up. I ran to the girl in the cage. Her eyes were closed and she didn't look well. I grabbed her wrist through the bars and felt for her pulse. To my relief, I found it, but it was so weak I could hardly believe she was still alive.

"This girl needs to get to a hospital right now," I yelled.

"I'm sorry, but I can't do that," Asta said. She had followed me down the stairs.

"Are you insane? She'll die."

"That was kind of the point of it all," Asta said.

I looked at her, perplexed. "Why? Why would you want to kill a young girl?"

As I asked the question, I received the answer on my own. My eyes fell on a big doll in the corner of the basement. As big as a human kid. I gasped and went closer to it to better see it. I had seen that girl before, I thought. Could it be? I studied it closely and touched its face. The eyes were different, replaced with plastic eyes, but the rest...I backed up and felt my stomach turn. Could it be? Was this really?

"This...this doll. This looks a lot like a real child. A child I have seen in a picture. A child that went missing in 2005," I said and looked at Asta for an explanation. I don't know what I wanted from her, what I expected, but somehow I really wanted her to say that I wasn't right, that this...this doll wasn't Helle's daughter.

Asta smiled and nodded. "Isn't she a beauty?"

I fought hard to control my breath and not hyperventilate. "So, that's what you were planning on doing to Josephine?"

Asta smiled. "In this way, they'll stay with me forever. They won't walk into the ocean and drown."

I suddenly realized how insane this woman really was, and wondered if I would be able to make it out of there alive.

That was when a third party joined the festivities. As if things weren't strange enough already, someone came walking down the stairs wearing a big grin on his face.

It was Patrick.

62

APRIL 2013

I couldn't believe my eyes. What was he doing here? The most prominent TV host in the country. It felt like a dream...a surrealistic, messed up dream.

"Isn't this nice?" he said.

"Who are you and what are you doing in my house?" Asta said angrily. "You have no right to be here."

"Well, I beg to differ," Patrick said.

He seemed to be enjoying this a little too much, I thought.

"Don't you know who this is?" I asked.

Asta shook her head.

"He's the host of the TV show *Shooting Stars*. His name is Patrick. Still doesn't ring a bell?"

"No. I don't watch TV. Besides, I don't care who he is or if he is the Crown Prince himself. He has no right to invade my house and neither have you. Now, all of you get out before I call the police."

I looked at her thinking she was truly mad. She sincerely believed she was the one who needed help from the police.

"Not so fast," Patrick said. He looked at Asta and then back at me again. "Now, this is perfect, isn't it?"

I didn't understand where he was going with this. All I could think about was the poor girl in the cage and how to get her out of there alive. "This girl needs to be taken to the hospital," I said.

Patrick tilted his head and grinned. "The Good Samaritan, huh? Well, I think it is truly perfect that you two are down here, even though it would be better with three...well, we could always count the dying girl in the cage, couldn't we? Then it would be almost right. See, I always wanted to make this like the scene in *Lace*, you know, Lucinda Lace. That glorious scene where Elizabeth Lace turns to look at her three possible mothers and asks them: Which one of you BITCHES is my mother?"

I stared at Patrick, feeling even more like it was all just a strange dream. "What?" I asked. "What the heck are you talking about? This girl is sick and needs medical attention and you're talking movies?"

Patrick raised a finger to stop me. "Mini-series. Not a movie. There's a DIFFERENCE, people."

Great. He had lost it, too. Maybe he'd always been crazy. Maybe he wasn't just acting on TV. Maybe he was as mad as they said. Asta took a step backwards, then started gasping for air. She stared at Patrick like he was a ghost.

"What are you talking about? Who is your mother? It makes no sense, Patrick," I said, then looked at Asta, who was still gasping for air while holding a hand to her chest.

"Well, it's not that I don't know which one of you is actually my mother, I just thought it would be a cool line to say," Patrick said.

That was when it finally hit me. "You're Asta's son?"

Patrick grinned again. Then he giggled like a schoolgirl. Asta stared at him in disbelief.

"No," she said. "It can't be? How can it be?"

"Oh, my God," I said, as the rest of the puzzle finally came together. "You're Nina? I mean you used to be Nina? You're a girl?"

"Gotcha!" Patrick said.

"I can't believe it," Asta said. Her voice was getting thick now. "You've come back? My little girl? Nina? My...my...Baby doll?"

Patrick's eyes sparkled with fire as he heard the last words. "Don't call me that! You gave away the right to call me that ever again when you gave me away to those horrible people."

"Gave you away?" Asta looked confused. "I don't understand. I didn't give you away. I would never give you away."

"Yes! Yes, you did. They told me so themselves. They all told me you didn't want me anymore, that you had sent me away because you couldn't handle me anymore. And I hate you for doing that. I loathe you for leaving me with those people."

"I don't understand. Nina, you must—"

"Patrick. I'm Patrick now. Nina is gone."

Asta moaned; she bent over, holding a hand to her stomach. "I can't...This is too much...I don't...I don't understand. They told me you had drowned, Nina. The police told me you had walked down to the beach and walked into the water thinking you could make it to the small island, but then the tides must have taken you. We searched for days for you. I thought you were dead. I swear."

He shook his head. "I don't believe you. You destroyed my life." He pointed at her with a shaking finger. His voice was trembling. "If only you knew what I went through, how I was... how I was abused. All those men, groping me, touching me in places I didn't even know I had, telling me I wasn't worth more than that, that my mother had abandoned me so they could teach me a lesson, teach me how to behave."

Asta held a hand to her chest. I could tell she was in pain and ran towards her. I managed to grab her just as she fainted. Patrick stared at her, then at me.

"Help me, Patrick. It looks like a heart attack. We need to get her and the girl to the hospital."

63

APRIL 2013

Patrick felt confused. He was staring at the woman and his mother, who was unconscious on the floor, not quite knowing what to do next. The woman knew who he was, so he had to kill her, of course. And his mother as well, since that was the entire purpose of coming here in the first place. But, somehow, it just didn't seem satisfying enough. His mother wasn't even awake to feel the pain that he had been looking forward to inflicting upon her for so very long. It just wasn't right. It wasn't how it was supposed to be.

Patrick moaned and stared at the woman who was trying to perform CPR on his mother. She knew who he was, so maybe he should just do her and then let the other two die on their own, a natural death. Get out of here before he was caught. Maybe stab his mother once or twice, just to make sure she was really dead. It wasn't the perfect scenario that he had wanted, but it was the best he could get right now.

Patrick exhaled. Oh, how it annoyed him to not get things his way. He wouldn't get the same rush out of it now that he was hoping for. This was supposed to be his big fix, his big moment, and now look at this?

"You know I have to kill you, don't you?" he mumbled, but the woman didn't hear him.

The woman breathed air into his mother's mouth, then pumped her heart. Patrick walked closer.

It doesn't matter if you bring her back or not. You're both gonna die. Patrick stopped. *That's it*, he thought. *That's the way to do it. Let the woman bring her back to life, and then when they both think it's all good, you kill them both.*

Patrick giggled at the thought and walked closer.

"She's breathing," the woman said with a sigh of relief.

"Good," Patrick said. He walked closer to his mother, who was coughing and moaning on the floor. The woman beside her looked at him with big eyes. "But we need to get her to a hospital right away."

Patrick bit his lip, then he shook his head. "No," he said. "NO! This wasn't how it was supposed to go. She was supposed to be mean and evil, and I was supposed to make her suffer. Stab her in the chest, then in the stomach, then look into her eyes as she drew her last breath," he said, and pulled out his butterfly knife. As he did, the small plastic bag with sewing kit and a bowtie fell onto the floor. He bent down and picked it up.

"Oh, my God," the woman said, and stared into his eyes. "You're the bowtie killer." Her eyes were filled with fear and Patrick finally felt the kick he had been searching for. He leaned over and started laughing.

"Don't hurt us," the woman pleaded with a shivering voice. "Please."

Patrick knelt next to his darling mother, who was fighting hard to breathe. Then he lifted the knife in the air, getting ready to stab her in the stomach, and hopefully crush and lacerate some of her organs. That was how he always did it. He always tried to not kill them right away. He liked inflicting pain, letting them suffer for a while before he stabbed them again, letting them know who was in charge, who was deciding if they should live or die. He smiled at the thought of finally being able to punish his mother for what she had done to him. He still didn't believe her little display of innocence. No, it was all just an act, it had to be. And Patrick knew all about acting. His mother looked at him and he finally saw the fear he had longed for in her eyes. It felt better than he had hoped it would.

"Please," she mumbled between coughs. "Please, don't."

"You sent me to hell, now I'm going to teach you what I learned there," Patrick said, imitating Elizabeth Lace once again.

As he got ready to stab his mother, he sensed movement behind him and turned just in time to see the dog jump towards him. Patrick screamed as the dog bit his arm and the knife clattered to the ground.

He watched as the woman got up and grabbed the knife from the ground. Now she was standing in front of him with it in her hand, shaking all over, threatening him while fumbling with her cellphone in the other hand. She looked completely ridiculous. Patrick clenched his fist and slammed it into the dog's head. Its eyes rolled back and it began to whimper before it finally let go of his arm.

Patrick heard the woman give the address over the phone. He considered for a second overpowering her and killing her right away, but the dog was getting back on its feet now, and it had started growling at him. Patrick then decided it was time to leave. He sprang for the stairs and ran through the living room and into the street. In the distance, he could hear sirens, as he put the hood over his head and disappeared into the darkness, cursing the woman and the dog, deciding to kill them as soon as he got the chance, which wouldn't be long, given the fact that they were on a small island. With a little luck, the police wouldn't believe her right away. It would at least take a while before they came for him, and by then he would be gone. He would vanish like he was an expert at doing.

But first he had a show to do. His last and final show, *le grand finale*.

64

———————

APRIL 2013

I was in shock, completely out of it when Officer Morten arrived. He stormed into the basement and saw Josephine and Asta on the floor. The dog growled a little, but Asta managed to hush him with the little strength she had left.

"Doctor Williamsen is on his way with the ambulance," he said.

I told him the entire story, even though it sounded a little too crazy to be true as the words left my mouth. The ambulance arrived and took both of them to be flown by helicopter to the mainland, they told us. I felt so relieved that it was out of my hands and could only hope that they would both survive. Officer Morten called the police in Esbjerg and told them to take care of Asta Kristensen and make sure she didn't leave the hospital.

Then, he looked at me. "Patrick, you say? *The* Patrick? Well,

I'll be damned. If I didn't know you so well, I would say you were nuts, but I can see how it could make sense."

"So, what do we do now?" I asked.

"*We* don't do anything. I will. I'm gonna call the investigators working on this case; I do believe they're back on the island after questioning Helle. They told me they would be here for the big show tonight and to make sure the entire port was heavily guarded."

"The show," I said.

"You think Patrick is there?" Officer Morten asked.

I shrugged. "That would be kind of stupid, wouldn't it?"

"You never know with this guy, apparently. We'll find him wherever he is hiding. He can't run far. But you go home and stay with your family, you hear me?" he said.

"Loud and clear," I said, and didn't tell him I had actually promised my neighbor to be at the show and watch her daughter sing. Even if Patrick was stupid enough to go down there, there was no way he could ever touch me. The place was packed with police and they would be all over him as soon as he showed his face.

I took my car and drove directly down to the port. I parked on a street not far from the area where the concert was going to be held. As I walked towards the entrance, I texted Sophia and asked her where I could find her. I found her in the front, very close to the stage, where she was standing with Jack and her son Christoffer. I elbowed my way through the crowd and joined them.

"You're late," Sophia said.

"Has it started yet?" I asked.

"No," Sophia said and looked at her watch. "It was supposed to, though, like fifteen minutes ago."

I wondered if they were going to begin without Patrick or if they'd have to cancel it all if he didn't show up. "Did you see Maya here anywhere?" I asked and looked into the packed crowd. "She was supposed to come down here with a friend."

"No," Sophia said. "But I'm sure she's here somewhere."

"You'd think she would be here somewhere in the front," I said, and looked down the line of people, mostly teenage girls, who were screaming and looking desperately at the stage waiting for the show to begin. That was when I spotted Maya's friend Annika in the crowd up front. I looked and looked, but didn't see Maya anywhere. Maybe she had gone with some other friends, I thought. Maybe she had stayed at home? I texted my dad and received a quick answer that Maya had left the house at five to go to the show. My heart dropped. I scanned the area around her friend again. There were several other girls next to her that she was talking to, but none of them were Maya.

"I have to check something," I said to Sophia, and started elbowing my way towards Maya's friend. "Excuse me. Excuse me, coming through."

I stared at Annika. "Where is Maya?" I yelled, trying to outshout the screaming crowd. The girl leaned over and yelled back,

"She's meeting Patrick. He promised to take her backstage."

The blood in my veins froze. I stared at the girl. She was blowing bubbles with her gum. "Are you sure about that?" I asked, my voice shaking with fear. "A hundred percent. She didn't even ask him if I could go, too. Way to be a good friend."

As Annika spoke the last words, music blared from the stage, and the light was turned on. A horrifying green light bathed the entire stage and an announcer started yelling.

"Are you ready to rock? Are you ready for *Shooooting Stars?* Ladies and gentlemen, let's get this party started. *Heeeeere's* Patrick."

The crowd went ballistic and I watched with my heart in my throat as Patrick entered into the green light that made him look as diabolic as I knew he was. But to my horror, he wasn't alone on stage. He had his arm around someone's neck.

It was Maya.

APRIL 2013

"**H**ELLOOOO **F**ANOE!" **P**ATRICK YELLED IN HIS MICROPHONE.

The crowd answered with gusto. *"Hello, Patrick."* A girl standing next to me screamed so loud it hurt my ear. Some were even crying while reaching their hands up towards him, like they believed they could touch him. I stared at Maya with my heart pounding. She was smiling a shy little smile.

"Fanoe!" he yelled. "This is Maya. Isn't she beautiful?"

The crowd screamed again. Most of them yelled yes, while others simply just screamed. I felt sick. I wanted to jump onto the stage and stop this madness right now, save my daughter from the grip of this lunatic before it was too late. I looked to find a police officer, but all I could see were security guards, who probably would never believe my story. Where were the police? Why hadn't they arrested Patrick yet? What were they waiting for?

As I wondered, I received my answer. Two officers yelled and sprang up on stage. I recognized them as Officers Nyberg and Gammelgaard. They were aiming their guns at Patrick while walking towards him on the stage. Patrick grabbed Maya around the neck and held her tight. I gasped. Then he pulled out a knife and placed it on her throat.

"Patrick, you're under arrest. Drop the knife," one of the officers yelled. "The place is surrounded. You'll never get away from here."

Thinking it was all just a part of the opening act, the crowd screamed and started cheering for Patrick.

"Patrick, Patrick, Patrick."

I saw the fear in my daughter's eyes and it hurt like knives piercing my skin. My heart was racing, and I felt so incredibly helpless.

"Come any closer and the girl dies," Patrick yelled.

"Patrick, Patrick, Patrick."

The two officers stopped and lowered their guns. "Patrick," the older one said. "Let the girl go. She hasn't done anything to you. You've killed enough, don't you think? Let her go and we'll find a solution. We'll help you."

"Patrick, Patrick, Patrick."

The crowd began to grow silent, waiting for Patrick's answer. Patrick laughed manically. The crowd laughed too, then the cheering continued. By that point, I'd had enough. I climbed the barrier separating the crowd from the stage, and before the security guards could grab me, I climbed onto the stage. I screamed and silenced the crowd, who was now beginning to realize this maybe wasn't part of some act or a part of the show after all.

"Patrick! Let my daughter go."

Patrick laughed when he saw me, then tightened his hold on Maya, who was now whimpering and crying. "So, this is your daughter, huh? Well, that's just PERFECT, isn't it? Now I simply HAVE to kill her."

That was when the crowd finally realized what was going on. Some screamed out of fear, while others started yelling at Patrick. A man threw a shoe at the stage and hit Patrick on the arm.

"*Let the girl go!*" he yelled. Then the rest of the crowd followed and started yelling at Patrick. "*Let her go. Let her go.*"

Patrick's face went red with anger. "No!" he yelled.

"*Let her go. Let her go.*"

"Screw you!" Patrick yelled and flipped them. But it didn't work any longer. Not now that he was actually giving them the finger and not just the media. Some people started booing. The rest of the crowd soon followed. Some were still chanting.

"*Let her go. Let her go.*"

Patrick was fuming with anger now. "NO," he yelled at them. "You love me, remember? I'm Patrick. You scream for me; you love me."

"*We hate you, Patrick,*" someone yelled from the crowd. The crowd applauded and cheered.

"*We hate you. We hate you,*" they chanted.

Patrick looked truly perplexed. He looked out at the people chanting and tried to yell back, but no one could hear him anymore. He was drowned out by the booing and the chanting.

Then something happened that I had not seen coming. At first, it was just the guy who had thrown the shoe who crawled up the stage, but soon hundreds of people followed him and literally stormed the stage. They ran towards Patrick with such speed and force that he didn't even manage to react. They pulled Maya out of his hands and overpowered Patrick. Maya ran into my arms crying, and I held her tight while tears rolled down my cheeks.

"Are you alright?" I said and stroked her cheeks gently.

She sniffled and nodded.

Right before Maya and I jumped off the stage, I looked back to cast one last glimpse at Patrick getting what he deserved. I heard him scream from somewhere inside the crowd of people, but I could no longer see him.

"I wanted to be the one to tell you this," Officer Morten said on the phone. I was sitting in my living room with my family. My dad was playing a game with Maya and Victor on the floor and was smiling and laughing for the first time in days.

I smiled and walked into the kitchen to better hear what he was telling me over the phone. I sat down. "Okay, I'm ready. What is it?"

"Well, first of all, I think that after this you'll have plenty of material for a new book," he said.

My eyes grew big and wide. "You've got my attention."

"You were right. All the children that disappeared were kidnapped. They didn't drown as we thought at first."

"Have you got evidence to back that up?" I asked.

"Yes. Polish police just dismantled a ring of trafficking criminals working together all over Europe. They arrested a guy who told them that back in the late nineties he had people helping him get young girls from Scandinavia to take them to Poland, where he sold them to different brothels. Scandinavian girls are worth a lot down there with their blonde hair and fair skin. But anyway, he had a contact in Denmark who worked out of Fanoe. The contact spotted girls around six years of age, blonde and with blue eyes, and stole them. Lured them with free ice cream from an ice cream truck at the playground. Then the contact would drive them across the border and into Germany, where the girls were picked up by eastern European men and brought into Poland to whomever would buy them. Patrick, who was Nina back then, was the first to be taken like this. He told his story himself when he was interrogated and finally broke down. The Fanoe contact worked for them in the years between 1997 and 1999 and was paid huge sums of money for each child."

"Wow," I said. "That's some story. I have a feeling you also know who this contact was?"

"I do, and that's what is a little unpleasant for you and your father."

"Helle," I said.

"Yes, I'm afraid so. We confronted her with this and she denied everything, but the money in her account speaks to her guilt. Plus, Patrick has identified her as the one who kidnapped him back then. We're guessing she stopped when she became pregnant with her own child. It was the same year that the disappearances stopped."

"That sounds plausible. But that means..." I paused and let the final pieces fall into place. "That Helle took Asta's daughter and sold her and..."

"Asta took Helle's daughter and stuffed her like a deer, yes.

Asta didn't know it was Helle who had taken her daughter. She lost it after losing her daughter and was desperate to get her back. She started making dolls, but none of them seemed real enough. Then she saw Helle's daughter one day and something went click inside of her. She convinced herself it was her Nina. Helle's daughter looked a lot like Nina, and she tells us that she knew she wasn't Nina to begin with, but somehow she wanted her to be so badly that she started believing she was actually her. She killed her and stuffed her to be able to keep her forever. It was the same with Josephine. When she saw her in the water, she was convinced it was Nina that had come home. Asta had been searching for her daughter ever since sensing that she was still alive, which was right, I guess."

I leaned back in my chair with a sigh. I heard my dad laugh in the living room and Maya whine with joy.

"What about the other kids that were stolen?" I asked.

Officer Morten sighed. "Polish police are helping us to try to track them down, but no luck so far. We have notified the parents and they're trying to raise money to conduct searches themselves."

"Both Asta and Josephine are being released from the hospital tomorrow. Asta will go to jail and so will Helle and Patrick."

"Hmm. I'm not sure anyone will ever believe me if I write this story, though."

"Then make it fiction," Officer Morten said, and laughed. "Listen, I gotta go. Let me know if you need anything else. For your book or...well, or maybe if you'd like to have dinner some time."

"Well, Officer Morten. I guess I'll think about that."

"You do that, Emma. See you around."

"See you."

I hung up and walked into the living room, where Maya was tickling my dad making him scream and whine like a schoolgirl. They stopped when they saw me.

"Victor, you should be in bed now. Go upstairs and get ready. I'll be up to tuck you in later."

"Who was that?" my dad asked.

I sighed, wondering if I should tell him the truth, tell him everything about Helle. I was about to do it, when Maya suddenly screamed.

"We're missing it." She sprang for the remote control and turned on the TV. "It's the new show everybody's talking about. It is *aaawesome*. They say the host is so gorgeous. I saw pictures of him online. Oh, my God. You won't believe it."

I looked at my dad, who shrugged. "You wanna go in the kitchen and grab a beer?" I asked.

"Anything beats having to watch another show on TV with some host acting crazy," my dad said.

My daughter scoffed and threw herself on the couch. "Old people. They just don't get it."

The End

———

Want to know what happens next? Get the next novel in the Emma Frost Mystery series here: Run, Run, as Fast as You Can

AFTERWORD

Dear Reader,

Thank you for purchasing *Miss Polly Had a Dolly*. It is the second book in my Emma Frost Mystery series. If you haven't read the first, *Itsy, Bitsy Spider*, then you can get it, and all of my other books by following the links below.

If you enjoyed this book, you might also enjoy my newest release *What Hurts the Most*; it takes place in Florida. You can read an excerpt from the novel on the following pages.

If you'd really like to help me out, then leave an honest review of this book where you bought it. Don't forget to like me on Facebook or follow me on twitter or my blog. I love getting mail from readers, so don't be shy about contacting me.

Take care,
Willow

To be the first to hear about new releases and bargains—from Willow Rose—sign up below to be on the VIP List. (I promise not to share your email with anyone else, and I won't clutter your inbox.)

- Sign up to be on the VIP LIST here :
http://readerlinks.com/l/415254

Tired of too many emails? Text the word: "willowrose" to 31996 to sign up to Willow's VIP text List to get a text alert with news about New Releases, Giveaways, Bargains and Free books from Willow.

Follow Willow Rose on BookBub:
https://www.bookbub.com/authors/willow-rose

Connect with Willow online:

https://www.amazon.com/Willow-Rose/e/B004X2WHBQ
https://www.facebook.com/willowredrose/
https://twitter.com/madamwillowrose
http://www.goodreads.com/author/show/
4804769.Willow_Rose
Http://www.willow-rose.net
madamewillowrose@gmail.com

ABOUT THE AUTHOR

Willow Rose is a multi-million-copy best-selling Author and an Amazon ALL-star Author of more than 60 novels. Her books are sold all over the world.

She writes Mystery, Thriller, Paranormal, Romance, Suspense, Horror, Supernatural thrillers, and Fantasy.

Willow's books are fast-paced, nail-biting pageturners with twists you won't see coming. That's why her fans call her The Queen of Scream.

Several of her books have reached the Kindle top 10 of ALL books in the US, UK, and Canada. She has sold more than three million books all over the world.

Willow lives on Florida's Space Coast with her husband and two daughters. When she is not writing or reading, you will find her surfing and watch the dolphins play in the waves of the Atlantic Ocean.

To be the first to hear about new releases and bargains—from Willow Rose—sign up below to be on the VIP List. (I promise not to share your email with anyone else, and I won't clutter your inbox.)

- Sign up to be on the VIP LIST here :
http://readerlinks.com/l/415254

Tired of too many emails? Text the word: "willowrose" to 31996 to sign up to Willow's VIP text List to get a text alert with news about New Releases, Giveaways, Bargains and Free books from Willow.

Follow Willow Rose on BookBub:
https://www.bookbub.com/authors/willow-rose

Connect with Willow online:

https://www.amazon.com/Willow-Rose/e/B004X2WHBQ
https://www.facebook.com/willowredrose/
https://twitter.com/madamwillowrose
http://www.goodreads.com/author/show/4804769.Willow_Rose
Http://www.willow-rose.net
madamewillowrose@gmail.com

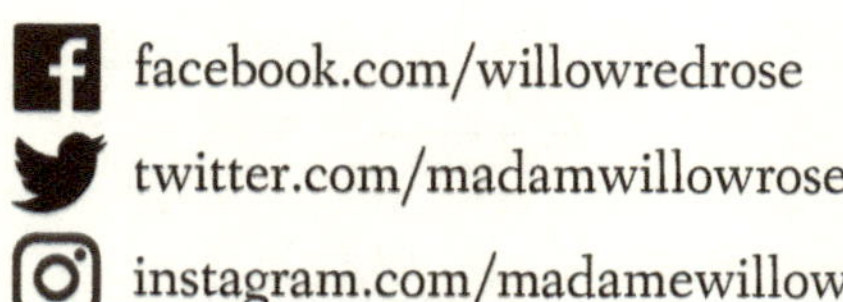

- Itsy Bitsy Spider
- Miss Dolly had a Dolly
- Run, Run as Fast as You Can
- Cross Your Heart and Hope to Die
- Peek-a-Boo I See You
- Tweedledum and Tweedledee
- Easy as One, Two, Three
- There's No Place like Home
- Slenderman
- Where the Wild Roses Grow
- Waltzing Mathilda
- Drip Drop Dead
- Black Frost

JACK RYDER SERIES

- Hit the Road Jack
- Slip out the Back Jack
- The House that Jack Built
- Black Jack
- Girl Next Door
- Her Final Word
- Don't Tell

REBEKKA FRANCK SERIES

- One, Two...He is Coming for You
- Three, Four...Better Lock Your Door
- Five, Six...Grab your Crucifix

- Seven, Eight...Gonna Stay up Late
- Nine, Ten...Never Sleep Again
- Eleven, Twelve...Dig and Delve
- Thirteen, Fourteen...Little Boy Unseen
- Better Not Cry
- Ten Little Girls
- It Ends Here

MYSTERY/THRILLER/HORROR NOVELS

- In One Fell Swoop
- Umbrella Man
- Blackbird Fly
- To Hell in a Handbasket
- Edwina

HORROR SHORT-STORIES

- Mommy Dearest
- The Bird
- Better watch out
- Eenie, Meenie
- Rock-a-Bye Baby
- Nibble, Nibble, Crunch
- Humpty Dumpty

- Chain Letter

———

PARANORMAL SUSPENSE/ROMANCE NOVELS

- In Cold Blood
- The Surge
- Girl Divided

THE VAMPIRES OF SHADOW HILLS SERIES

- Flesh and Blood
- Blood and Fire
- Fire and Beauty
- Beauty and Beasts
- Beasts and Magic
- Magic and Witchcraft
- Witchcraft and War
- War and Order
- Order and Chaos
- Chaos and Courage

THE AFTERLIFE SERIES

- Beyond
- Serenity
- Endurance
- Courageous

THE WOLFBOY CHRONICLES

- A Gypsy Song
- I am WOLF

DAUGHTERS OF THE JAGUAR

- Savage
- Broken

Cover design by Juan Villar Padron,
https://juanjjpadron.wixsite.com/juanpadron

Special thanks to my editor Janell Parque
http://janellparque.blogspot.com/

———

To be the first to hear about new releases and bargains from Willow Rose, sign up below to be on the VIP List. (I promise not to share your email with anyone else, and I won't clutter your inbox.)

- Tap here to sign up to be on the VIP LIST -

Tired of too many emails? Text the word: "willowrose" to 31996 to sign up to Willow's VIP text List to get a text alert with news about New Releases, Giveaways, Bargains and Free books from Willow.

Connect with Willow online:
Facebook
Twitter
GoodReads
willow-rose.net
madamewillowrose@gmail.com

CONTENTS

www.ingramcontent.com/pod-product-compliance
Lightning Source LLC
Chambersburg PA
CBHW021302190726
48288CB00003B/655